Jessica looked great

Perhaps a bit curvier than he remembered, but heck, at the time he hadn't been paying as much attention to the form as the opportunity. "Everybody eats more at the holidays."

She nodded slowly, her eyes holding his.

Zach's heart began to beat hard in his chest, nearly stealing his breath, almost painfully choking it from him. "You wouldn't be trying to tell me in your refined way that you're...eating more because you're eating for two. Would you?"

Her gaze dropped for just an instant, but in that instant he knew that he had followed in his brother Duke's footsteps. "I'll be damned," he murmured, trying to sort out how he felt. Delighted, devastated, shocked, scared—

"Actually, three," she said quietly, her eyes moving back to catch his.

He blinked. "Three what?"

She shrugged. "I'm eating for three. Me and the twins. Merry Christmas, Zach."

Dear Reader,

I love holiday stories! They are one of my favorite things to write because, for me, the underlying themes of the season are family, friends and tradition. No matter what your faith or nationality, each person knows the beauty of spending time with their loved ones against a rich and varied tapestry of tradition. And a holiday story is a chance to relive all those wonderful emotions!

I hope you'll enjoy the story of Zach Forrester and Jessica Tomball Farnsworth, two very different personalities from opposite walks of life. I believe that Christmas works its magic on the most stubborn people, and magic even in the most challenging of circumstances can bring love to the most impossible situation. May your holiday season be lit by this very special spirit of love, charity and fulfillment.

Best wishes and much love,

Tina Leonard

Tina Leonard
THE CHRISTMAS TWINS

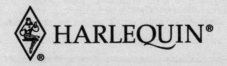

HARLEQUIN®

TORONTO • NEW YORK • LONDON
AMSTERDAM • PARIS • SYDNEY • HAMBURG
STOCKHOLM • ATHENS • TOKYO • MILAN • MADRID
PRAGUE • WARSAW • BUDAPEST • AUCKLAND

ISBN-13: 978-0-373-75141-9
ISBN-10:   0-373-75141-9

THE CHRISTMAS TWINS

Copyright © 2006 by Tina Leonard.

This edition published by arrangement with Harlequin Books S.A.

® and TM are trademarks of the publisher. Trademarks indicated with ® are registered in the United States Patent and Trademark Office, the Canadian Trade Marks Office and in other countries.

www.eHarlequin.com

Printed in U.S.A.

ABOUT THE AUTHOR

Tina Leonard loves to laugh, which is one of the many reasons she loves writing Harlequin American Romance books. In another lifetime Tina thought she would be single and an East Coast fashion buyer forever. The unexpected happened when Tina met Tim again after many years—she hadn't seen him since they'd attended school together from first through eighth grade. They married, and now Tina keeps a close eye on her school-age children's friends! Lisa and Dean keep their mother busy with soccer, gymnastics and horseback riding. They are proud of their mom's "kissy books" and eagerly help her any way they can. Tina hopes that readers will enjoy the love of family she writes about in her books. A reviewer once wrote, "Leonard had a wonderful sense of the ridiculous," which Tina loved so much she wants it for her epitaph. Right now, however, she's focusing on her wonderful life and writing a lot more romance! You can visit her at www.tinaleonard.com.

Books by Tina Leonard

HARLEQUIN AMERICAN ROMANCE

"TULIPS SALOON" COCONUT CAKE

Prepare white cake from scratch or a mix (the kind with pudding in the mix is best). Frost with white icing (recipe below) and then generously sprinkle with shredded coconut. Use frozen coconut if possible, but bagged will do.

Icing

Blend in mixer:

3 cups sifted confectioners' sugar
4 tbsp melted butter
2 or 3 tbsp condensed milk
3 oz softened cream cheese (more if you like)
2 tsp vanilla

~~~ Special thanks to Mercier Decuir

"I've tried to be perfect. I've lived in a world that wants perfect. Imperfect is a lot more fun."
—Jessica Tomball Farnsworth

Chapter One

Zach Forrester freely admitted that boredom was his worst enemy.

He didn't mind living in Tulips, Texas, on the Triple F ranch, but he wanted to do more in his life than just take care of a family property. He had plans to build a new elementary school in the small town, a challenge he would enjoy.

But now it was time for a different challenge. Maybe the late September moon was getting to him, but excitement seemed to be a hard-to-find commodity.

One thing was for certain, he wasn't giving up his life the way Duke had, to diapers and a wife and a round-cheeked baby. He loved his little nephew, but a baby put a certain stop to one's life. Nor would he ever let a woman lead him around by the nose as Liberty had Duke. She had left the altar with Duke standing at it, then made a surprise return with his baby, finally marrying Duke in a wonderfully romantic ceremony.

Of course, Duke was insanely happy with his new wife and child, but it had been hell on Duke getting there. Zach had to admit it had been fun watching his older brother struggle mightily to get his woman. *Everything always seems to come easy for my brother and sister and harder for me.*

He was enjoying his pity party as he drove, until he saw the hot pink convertible T-bird and the madwoman standing next to his favorite bull, which she'd clearly hit. She was talking on her cell phone as if it was just any old piece of meat she'd struck. But Brahma Bud was his best and finest!

Hopping out of his truck, Zach stared at the imperious woman with whiskey-colored hair. "What the hell do you think you're doing?"

She snapped her cell phone shut. "I am *trying* to get this beast to move, Cowboy. He seems to think he has the right of way."

"He does!" Zach stared at his poor bull, which gazed back in return, not bothered in the least by the annoying woman who had hit him.

"Well, he's been having his way for an hour,"

she replied, her voice so haughty it belonged in New York. "Do you think you could move his plump hide?"

Perhaps Brahma Bud had only been lightly tapped, because the bull didn't seem any worse for wear. He did, however, seem quite mesmerized by the pink T-bird, and as Zach forced himself to calm down, he had to admit the car—and the woman— were definitely worth second looks. "What's the rush, City?"

"I have a life," she told him. "I just can't stand here and watch the grass grow."

Well, hell, Zach thought, wasn't she special. Of course, she certainly looked special in her tight dress. When she spoke, she emphasized her words so that all of her bounced in the right places. "He might move tomorrow," Zach said. "Once he gets to a spot he likes, he tends to stay there."

"You have *got* to be kidding me!" she exclaimed, enunciating and bouncing, to Zach's delight.

Ah, city folk. So much fun. He leaned against her T-bird and gave her his best leer. "When I get to a spot I like, I tend to stay there, too."

"Cowboy, I know all about guys like you, and believe me, the words are bigger than the deed. Just take your cow and go home, okay? And I won't charge you for the dent in my fender. Not to mention I think he used his antler to lift my skirt when I tried to make certain he was all right."

"Yeah, that would be the easy way out," Zach said slowly, suddenly realizing what he wanted more than anything was to shake things up, and this gal was a smoking-hot challenge even if she didn't know horns from antlers. "I'll do two things for you—one, I'll ask my prize longhorn here to move, if you're nice. Two, I won't ask why you're trespassing on my private drive, if you're nice. I won't even be mad that you hit my livelihood, here," he said, dropping a casual hand to Bud's horn. "However, I do insist upon a kiss."

She gasped. "I consider kissing to be sex. Why would I have sex with a stranger?"

He laughed out loud. "Make it a brotherly peck, then."

"No. You're weird. It might be catching."

"I think you're the weird one." Crossing his arms, he decided this exceptional woman was his next challenge. "So, I noticed you didn't protest that you had a boyfriend or were married or something."

She wrinkled her nose. "I just broke up with my boyfriend. He was too possessive."

Zach raised his brows. "Possessive?"

"He thought he owned me."

"Boyfriends will act like that sometimes." He wondered if he'd feel the same way if she was his girlfriend. *Nah.* He'd never felt that way about any woman. *Safe!*

Her back stiffened. "Being possessive is bad and being bossy is worse. But if you'd like to boss someone around, why don't you tell that cow to move so I can get back on the road?"

He shook his head. "You're not going anywhere."

She put her hands on her hips, prepared to give him a nor'easter full of cold sass. "Why not?"

"It's not just the fender you damaged. It's hanging off." He pointed to the front of her car. "And you have a flat tire. I notice you didn't respond to my offer of a kiss, by the way."

Jessica Tomball Farnsworth looked at the cowboy. He was hunky, to be sure, but so was her ex-fiancé. She'd learned that a man that hot was usually firing more than one pistol at a time—just as her possessive ex-boyfriend had. He'd found a more available set of female arms while she'd been away on business, traveling with her cosmetics company.

That thought led her to consider dropping straight into this willing man's arms and slathering his face with kisses since he wanted kissing so badly. After all, revenge was sweet.

But she felt a stronger desire to get as far away from men as possible. She wasn't bitter; she was simply willing to acknowledge that either she was a poor judge of character or all men were louses.

Until she had that figured out, she wasn't kissing this cowboy, or any male. She narrowed her eyes at him. *Make that hot cowboy.* "Smooth come-ons like yours put me off." Taking a deep breath for bravery, she gave the large animal a push on his rump to encourage him to move.

He swished his tail in response.

"We could be here all day," the cowboy said.

This seemed, unfortunately, to be true. She had places she needed to be. With her heart beating too fast, she rose on tiptoe and kissed the cowboy full on the mouth, more than ready to get the hell out of wherever she was.

He looked at her when she sank back to ground level.

"You call that a kiss?"

"Yes, I do," she said tartly. "Do you keep your promises or not?" A delicious zing of wonder had struck her when she'd brushed his lips, along with a wayward desire for more, more, more.

He took a peppermint from his pocket and let the giant bull smell it before tossing it into the winter-touched yellow meadow. The bull casually strolled after the candy treat while the man inspected the broken fence, which had allowed his beast to escape and wander the roadside. Never in her life had she seen an animal that big up close. But then its kind, curious eyes had stared over the hood at her, and she'd been grateful it didn't appear to be hurt.

"Why do you keep animals like that?" she asked. "He deserves to be wild and free."

The cowboy laughed. "He is wild and free, City. This is my best friend. He lives in the lap of luxury."

He was clearly amused by her lack of knowledge of his world. Jessica sniffed, not liking his attitude at all. "I suppose you think it's cute to give him candy. What happens when he gets a cavity?"

He sent a slow, amused grin her way. Shaking his head, he went to inspect her car.

Jessica ignored him, keeping her gaze on the bull, which appeared to be just as happy inside the meadow as out.

"What's your name?"

"Jessica," she said, unwilling to share more.

"Mine's Zach," he replied, though she hadn't asked. "I can help you get on your way, Jessie."

She turned, staring at him.

"Or you could kiss me again," he said conversationally. "I know you liked it as much as I did."

She gasped. "No. I didn't."

He smiled, the expression in his dark eyes registering disbelief. It made Jessica mad that he knew better, and madder to know she was so easy to read.

"So," he said, drawing near to her, "was it good sex?"

Not as good as it could be. "I'll thank you to not make fun of my sense of decency," Jessica said. "Thank you for stopping and moving your cow out of the way. Now please tell me where I can get this tire fixed."

"You certainly have issues, lady," Zach said, catching her hand in his, "but I'm not afraid of issues. In fact, I look forward to helping you solve yours, Jessie." He ran a thumb over her bottom lip. "Tell me your full name."

"Jessica Tomball Farnsworth," she whispered, wondering why she bothered to answer. "I don't have as many issues as you do, by the way." She backed away, knowing full well he was messing with her senses.

"Sure I do, City," he said, moving closer. "Where I come from, a man's not a man unless he's got a full plate of issues. Sins." He gave her a wink and slid a hand around her waist. "We're born with issues, and we use them to lure women 'cause they think they can save us from ourselves. Then we die with our issues, knowing we've enjoyed them every step of the way."

"You're crazy," she whispered, unable to make her escape because of the way he was pressing her against the car.

"And you like it," he said against her neck, shifting his hands under her Versace skirt.

"I think I do," Jessica said, closing her eyes. *What the hell. I was never cut out for boredom.*

And Jessie T., boyfriend-dumper and responsibility-escaper dragged the bad boy into the back seat of her hot pink T-bird, embracing sins and issues and everything else that came with the sinfully hot package.

Chapter Two

Two hours later, Zach stared up at the sun in the Texas sky from the back seat of the T-bird, glad his ranch was off the beaten path and that he'd had enough privacy to enjoy this wonderful surprise gift from the city.

Who said you couldn't find a city girl worth wasting country on, anyway?

He examined the blanket he'd found in the back seat. The label read Saks Fifth Avenue. "So I'm guessing you're on the pill," he said idly, wondering if he could talk the beautiful stranger into staying at his ranch for about another day. Only his sister, Pepper, was ever around the ranch anymore, and she pretty much kept to herself. "Ow!"

He rubbed the spot on his cheek where City

had slapped him. It had actually been a light tap, but it was enough to get his attention.

She stared at him, angry again, reminding him that her spirit was one of the many things he liked about her. "So are you?" he asked, thinking with some trepidation about Liberty and Duke and their unplanned pregnancy.

"You are not a gentleman!" Jessie exclaimed. He nodded, and said, "We already established that. Let's get to the answer."

Her cheeks pinked. "I use a method of control."

He glared. "Don't they discuss birth control where you're from?" He glanced at the blanket label again. "Saks Fifth Avenue?"

She ignored him.

Okay. She obviously didn't want to talk about it. A faint trickle of unease slithered through him.

"I have to go," she said abruptly. "Please get the hell out of my car."

He frowned. "Not until you tell me about your 'method.'"

"You should have asked before," she said. "No matter what my method is, if it's not any good, it's too late."

He digested that, realizing she was right. Had he lost his mind? His gaze ran over her tight, smooth skin. The luscious curves had bewitched him, and all of her attitude set off raging emotions inside him.

Duke must have felt just this way about Liberty.

He had never wanted to be like Duke, despite the fact that, to him, his sheriff brother was pretty much a hero in all ways. If not a hero, then a major example of what a good man should be.

But he'd never wanted to be out-of-his-mind wild over a woman, and he sure as hell had never wanted to get one pregnant out of wedlock.

That would spell commitment for certain, and he hated everything about the sound of that particular word.

"I've been seeing twins," he murmured, going for jackass and making it pretty well, he thought. That should run her off quicker than wildfire, which he needed her to do if he was going to escape this growing dilemma and the future his brain was imagining.

"I don't care," she said, laughing, "if you're dating triplets. Or quadruplets."

He scratched his chin, noticing she wasn't leaping out of the back seat. In fact, they felt rather companionable together, their legs stretched out along the soft leather. She fit him very well. "Got a sister?" he asked, trying to save himself.

She gave him a thorough eyeing. "Really working those issues, aren't you?"

She wasn't falling for it. Women always fell for his routine! Jessie got out of the car, fixed her skirt and hair and pulled a huge carpetbag-sized purse from the front seat. She rummaged around in it, fishing out a pair of red panties. "Close your eyes."

"I can't," he said. "Watching you is the most fun I've had lately."

She shrugged, reaching under her skirt to shimmy her lacy panties into place. He felt himself wanting her again. She had impossibly long legs and nothing he didn't want to see. She was an intriguing beauty, tempting his eyes. Silently, he handed her the panties he'd previously removed and tossed to the floor. She snatched them from him, stuffing them into the carpetbag.

The panties went into the carpetbag. He realized with a pang and a worrisome erection that she was used to traveling or undressing because most women didn't carry a change of underwear in their purse. "Don't suppose you're going to change your bra, too?"

She shook her head at his hopeful tone. "Hand me the one you took off."

It was soft and silky, like her. He wanted her where he could enjoy her for hours, without the top and skirt, which had been left on out of necessity. He'd been lucky to discard her bra and panties, actually, because he'd discovered she had a cute shy side despite her projected carefree attitude. "You're beautiful," he said, knowing she was that way without trying to be.

"It's my business," she said. "It's all a mirage."

There, he thought, *that's an answer to scare the hell out of even the baddest, bootwearing hardass around.*

Jessie was thinking through the birth control issue, more concerned than she was letting on. The truth was, she'd been fitted with a vaginal ring when she and her boyfriend had gotten serious enough to discuss marriage. But they hadn't had sex in the past couple of months, as he'd claimed to be working late—an excuse she was to learn was code for: *Your chief business rival and I aren't just discussing the latest spring palette after-hours.* So she hadn't been wearing the ring when she'd left the city and the man behind.

Babies had been the first thing on her agenda,

following a wedding. But there was no reason to tell that to Zach. He seemed like the worrying type. Any other man would have simply let her drive off into the sunset. Then again, he had issues, as he'd calmly and proudly admitted. She decided to keep her desire for a baby a secret. "I've got to go, cowboy," she said.

"My name is Zach," he said, sounding a bit cross about it.

She nodded. "I know."

"No, you didn't," he said. "Jessie T., you're not a good liar. You forgot my name."

She looked at him.

"You're not even on birth control, are you?"

He *was* going to be difficult. "Are *you?*" she asked, stalling for time. "Maybe you were wearing a condom and I didn't notice." She would have noticed, definitely, because it had been skin-on-skin passion, nothing between her and him in the most wonderful connection a man and woman could share.

His jaw set. "Great. This is my worst nightmare."

She didn't usually have a temper but irritation crept into her. *More like raging than creeping.* "It's none of your affair."

"Well, now," he said, his voice a stony drawl,

"that's where you're wrong, Miss Jessica. One thing about us Forresters is that we make everything our business. After you've been in Tulips for a while, you'll know this to be true." He snagged her car keys from the ignition. "Come on, city girl. No doubt you're going to make me crazy for the next month, but there's always a little hell to pay for a little pleasure."

She grabbed for the keys but he held them above her head. "You can't keep me here."

"I'm not keeping you," he said, scooping her up to deposit her into his truck bed. "Your car is out of commission."

"No, it's not," Jessie protested. She'd bitten off more than she could handle with him. Zach was nothing like her ex, a man easily led by his groin and whichever way the wind was blowing at the time: Blonde, brunette, redhead. "Look, you were a great fantasy, but—"

He stopped her in the act of crawling out of the truck bed. "If you're going to be easy about this, you can ride in the front seat. If you're going to be difficult, you ride in the back and I've got some throwing rope to make sure of it. But you leaving is not an option. It's one of my issues, you see."

He grinned at her. Jessie pressed her lips together. "I have a business convention I have to attend. It's really important. We're presenting holiday looks for the upcoming season. This being September, I've got to get the wares on the road."

"I sympathize." He nodded. "But you can clearly see that your car is leaking something."

Jessie stared at the ground in horror. Something was leaking from her precious T-bird!

"I can't have you running off around the world to Saks Fifth Avenue and the like if you're carrying my child."

"I'm not!"

He leaned against the truck, crossing his arms. "Let me share with you the problem. My brother fell in love with a woman, and they were supposed to get married. They were in the middle of getting married, in fact, but she got cold feet at the altar, and before we knew what was happening, Liberty went running off faster than a greased piglet in a pig race."

"That has nothing to do with me," Jessie said, trying to sound like she didn't care. However, she could see where Zach would empathize with his brother.

"Well, it turned out Liberty was pregnant," Zach continued, ignoring her, "though she didn't tell Duke. She was afraid to, and then the little old ladies in our town, and the men, too—you'll meet them all soon enough—well, the Tulips Saloon Gang got involved—"

"Gang?" Jessie whispered.

"Gang." Zach nodded. "You don't know anything about issues until you meet the Gang."

She blinked, not wanting to get drawn into this sexy man's loony life. "I'll call you if I'm pregnant."

"You wouldn't," Zach said. "And then I'd be like Duke almost was, with a son of mine wandering around out there, never knowing that his daddy was a caring man who wanted to play football with him and teach him to hunt and shoot beer cans. Budweiser beer cans only, which is how my great-horned beast out there got his name, Brahma Bud. I keep my life simple, as you'll learn."

"Oh, no," Jessie murmured, the impact of her flyaway good sense dawning on her. "Where is the rewind button on my life?"

IT WASN'T HEROIC of him to do what he was doing to the flitty woman who'd blown into town, but it wouldn't be fair if he had a son that never knew its father. Zach was quite satisfied that he'd made the best possible decision considering the circumstances.

His sister, Pepper, would tell him he should have kept his pants zipped, and he should have, but he didn't regret making love to that little firecracker out there staring sadly at her car, which had been towed to the drive of the Triple F Ranch. He watched Jessie through the window, smiling when the family dog—who was supposed to be Duke's dog but couldn't be trained to one person—greeted Jessie with a big doggie smile and a wave of a golden plumed tail. Her name was Molly, or Jimbo if other members of the town of Tulips were asked.

Zach grinned. Jessie knew nothing about issues until she met the citizens of Tulips. It was time to introduce her, even though he'd be painted as the black villain of the piece—a part which he'd relish, much as Duke had.

Actually, his older brother had suffered under the good-hearted critiquing of the town's elders. But Zach was prepared for it. He knew what he'd done—and he was prepared to pay the price.

He would take his critiquing in stride, because every time the elders tried to point out the error of his ways, he'd just think about Jessie's partially nude body and smile like Molly-Jimbo with a new bone.

"Oh, my," Pansy Trifle said when Zach walked through the heavy glass-and-wood doors of the Tulips Saloon.

Helen Granger stood, her hands on her hips. "This is Ladies Only Day, Zach."

"I know," he said, with a most regretful tone, to the room at large, "so I've brought you a lady." He tipped his hat to all of them, and gave Jessie a gentle push. "Take good care of my friend from Saks Fifth Avenue."

He left, a broad grin on his face. Very soon he would be in big trouble with the elders of the town, and he was going to enjoy being the cause of all the uproar.

In the meantime, he had a T-bird to "hide," just in case Ms. Saks decided to take a fast hike, à la Duke's wife, the cagey Ms. Liberty Wentworth.

History would not be repeating itself.

Chapter Three

Helen and Pansy stared at the newcomer with surprise, sympathy and curiosity. Nervously, Jessie said, "I'm not really from Saks."

The ladies in the room laughed.

"Sit down here," Ms. Pansy said, patting an antique chair. "Zach must want us to get to know you better or he wouldn't have brought you here."

"Which makes him even nuttier than we'd previously surmised," Helen said. "I'll get you a cup of tea while Pansy introduces you to everyone. Then we'll be more than happy to advise you on whatever problem that Forrester male is giving you."

Following some brief introductions, Jessica told her story. "Well, you see," Jessie said, after being introduced, "I hit his steer. Or maybe it was a bull. I'm not certain of the proper terminology."

Pansy looked at her. "Not Brahma Bud?"

"I'm afraid so."

"Oh, my," Helen said. "I do hope Bud's all right. Zach's had him since he was a child. Won't part with him."

Jessie blinked. "I didn't realize it was a pet."

"Well," Pansy said, "it was a gift from his parents. So it's a link with the past, you might say."

"I might have been a bit callous," Jessie said. "I might have called Bud a hunk of steak or something. I don't remember. I was very angry."

"Why were you angry, dear?" Pansy asked gently.

"I was in a hurry to get somewhere," Jessie said, "and the bull—do you call it a bull or a steer?"

"Not important," Helen said, dropping a lump of sugar into her teacup. "Continue, please."

Jessie sighed, realizing they didn't want to have to explain something to her that was plainly obvious to everyone in the room. "There are places I need to be. Bud stopped me. He wouldn't move. I thought maybe he was hurt or in shock, but I really barely tapped him. In fact, he did more damage to my car than I realized, because Zach said my car was leaking."

"Hmm." Pansy put some cookies on a plate for her. "We're so glad you've come to Tulips, dear."

"But we understand you want to be on your way." Helen smiled around at all the ladies in the gathering. "Are you staying with Pepper and Zach?"

"I don't want to," Jessie said. "Is there a hotel in town?"

"We'll have one in the future, I feel certain," Helen said. "Or at least a bed-and-breakfast."

Jessie shook her head. "My family isn't used to me being anything other than right on schedule."

They perked up. "Do tell us about your family," Pansy said.

"Well, my mother and father own a cosmetics company called Jessie's Girl Stuff. I have two brothers. They're lawyers," Jessie said.

"Lawyers," Pansy said, glancing at Helen.

Helen smiled at her. "Did you call them, dear?"

"I let them know where I was. And I told them I'd be on time for the convention in two days." Jessie took a deep breath. "Zach says I can't leave, though."

"Until your car is fixed," Helen said.

"Until…" Jessie paused, not about to admit her plight.

"Oh, my," Pansy said, "I do believe our Zach is developing feelings for you, Jessie."

Jessie's eyes went wide. "Just the opposite. He's quite pigheaded."

"Aren't they all?" Helen said with a smile. "Do you like him?"

"No," Jessie said. "Bossy men are not my thing."

"We completely understand." Pansy nodded. "So what we want you to do is call this number." She scribbled a number onto a tulip-printed pad and handed it to Jessie. "We have a few men in our town, very few, mind you, but the ones we have are mostly useless. I mean, *useful*."

"Yes," Helen agreed. "Ask to speak to Bug Carmine. He'll be more than happy to taxi you wherever you want to go. Where is this convention of yours, dear?"

"California," Jessie said. "Do you think it will take that long to fix my car?"

"You could call roadside assistance," Pansy said. "They'd probably be out here lickity-split and fix you right up."

Jessie straightened. Of course they would! "You ladies are marvelous! I never thought about that! I don't know why I didn't, except that I never hit a bull before—"

"And Zach swept you off your feet," Helen inserted.

"Yes, and that's never happened before, either. I mean, how many people hit a poor sweet animal like Brahma Bud… But roadside assistance is the perfect answer! Shame on Zach for saying you all had issues," Jessie said. "You're clearly as smart and capable as anyone I've ever met."

Helen sniffed, reaching for a cookie off the tray Pansy had set down. "Zach said *we* had issues?"

"Oh, yes," Jessie said, nodding. "He said I didn't even know the meaning of the word until I'd met 'the Gang.'"

"Well." Pansy smiled brightly. "Helen, dear, why don't you hand sweet Jessie the phone so she can make her call? I'll telephone Sheriff Duke while you're doing that, and let him know his baby brother needs his brotherly supervision."

Helen grinned and gave Jessie the old-fashioned, floral-painted phone.

"And if they can't fix your car today," Pansy said, "you're welcome to stay at my house for as long as you like." She and Helen shared a secretive and satisfied glance as Jessie dialed.

FAR FROM BEING SUPPORTIVE and helpful, Zach learned that the Gang wasn't going to be as conniving about him and Jessie as they'd been about Liberty and Duke. Much to his chagrin, they'd ratted him out to his brother about Jessie's presence at the ranch, earning him a lecture on propriety and a babysitter in the form of Pepper.

Pepper was the soul of responsibility. A hard-working student and now a much-lauded doctor, she was well respected not just in Tulips, but in the medical community. With Duke and Pepper on his case about his houseguest, Zach was certain he'd never feel the glory of Jessie's skin again.

But what had he expected from the Gang? They never operated the way one suspected they might. Now he understood why Duke had been so miserable as the object of their machinations.

Secretly, he'd hoped that they would try to encourage some type of romance between he and Jessie. He'd been looking, in fact, for some matchmaking by the little old ladies, and perhaps a bolstering of his worth in Jessie's eyes.

Something had gone terribly wrong. Jessie was now staying with Pansy, and Helen wouldn't speak to him. Duke was breathing down his neck, and even Molly hesitated to allow him to pet her.

He was in the proverbial doghouse, and it was a very uncomfortable place to be.

But a man had to stand firm. When the roadside assistance fellow came out to the Triple F ranch, Zach told him the car had been repaired and that he could leave. It was lucky he'd thought to hide Jessie's car in one of the outlying barns on the ranch.

"It's hard to be the villain," he told the chickens that were checking out the white-walled tires of Jessie's T-bird. "Being dishonorable is not fun. But if I let that gal out of my sight, I could very well end up worse than Duke."

He and Duke and Pepper had grown up in a traditional family. Liberty had been raised by parents who mainly ignored her, but luckily she'd lived nearby and had been befriended by Zach—who had always looked at her as a brother would—and by his parents. But her sad upbringing had hurt her all her life. He could never do that to a child of his own.

He sat on the bumper of Jessie's car. "I wish I could say I shouldn't have done it, but I liked being with her," he told Molly as she sat beside him, her golden fur soft and reassuring under his touch. "I liked being with Jessie more than I ever liked being with a woman in my life."

Molly barked at him.

"Yeah, it's crazy." He got off the bumper. "I just hope she's not as fertile as she looks, because as hard as it's been to keep her in Tulips, I'd likely never get her to the altar!"

JESSIE PUT her carpetbag away in Pansy's guest room, glad she always carried makeup and a change of clothes. She had a secret, one of many, only this one was a big one, and the cowboy had made her realize how much she didn't like hiding it.

She was afraid of settling down. She'd simply wanted a baby, and her ex-boyfriend had been the way to achieve that.

She'd come to the unhappy realization that she'd probably never been in love with him, which probably meant she was shallow and vain. Her family was successful; she shouldn't have needed to conjure up a relationship in order to validate her goals in life.

Maybe she was lacking a fundamental building block in her personality, like patience or strength of character. "Trust a relaxing jaunt through the country to give me more time to think and be hard on myself. Just what every second-thoughts bride needs."

She heard the doorbell ring as she put away her belongings. A second later, Pansy called, "Jessie!" up the stairwell.

Jessie walked down, surprised to see Zach sitting very properly in Pansy's living room. "Hi, Zach," she said, trying to ignore the excitement rushing through her.

Pansy sat down in a nearby chair and began to knit, a quiet chaperone. Jessie sat in a floral chair across from Zach.

Zach looked at her. "Settling in all right?"

Jessie nodded. "Yes, thank you. And I sent roadside assistance out to repair whatever was leaking on my car."

Zach shifted on the sofa. "Would you like to take a walk?"

Jessie shook her head. "I'm pretty tired. It's been a long day."

"Okay." Zach stood, nodding to Pansy. "See you all later."

He departed, surprising Jessie. She looked at Pansy as the door shut behind Zach.

"Oh," Pansy said. "I do think he likes you."

Jessie knew what was really on Zach's mind. "I don't think so. I just think he's very protective."

Pansy put away her knitting. "You know, it's been difficult for Zach. He's the middle child, and was often pushed to the side. Not quite the man of the house, and not the baby. Sometimes I thought he was never certain whether he wanted to follow in Duke's footsteps or be a role model for Pepper. He tried to do both and somewhere along the line, he became a bit arrogant and somewhat overly determined."

"I can see where women would be attracted to that trait."

"Yes," Pansy said with a smile, "but he's never bothered to ask any of them to take a walk."

Jessie shook her head. It didn't matter. She was leaving as soon as her car was fixed. There were enough stray matters in her life to occupy her time. "Thankfully my car might be repaired tomorrow. Good night, Pansy. Thank you for everything."

Pansy waved a hand as Jessie stood. "I'm enjoying having you here, Jessie. Plan on staying as long as you like."

Until the morning, Jessie thought. *And then I'm out of here.*

Before she was waylaid by the temptation of an attentive, opinionated cowboy who had "bad for you" written all over him.

JESSIE SLEPT WELL. In the morning she showered, ate breakfast with Pansy and Helen—scones and hot tea—packed her carpetbag and hitched a ride in Sheriff Duke Forrester's truck to the Triple F.

"If my brother gives you any more trouble," Duke said, "you just let me know. I'll give him a pounding he'll never forget. Or better yet, just tell Pepper. Zach hates it when Pepper gets on to him."

"That won't be necessary." Jessie smiled. "My car should be fixed by now, and I'll be out of everyone's hair."

"Well," Duke said, "if you ever want a place to visit, I know the ladies would love to have you back. They're always trying to entice people to settle here."

"Oh." Jessie looked out at the passing country-side. "It's pretty here, but—"

"Not your kind of place," Duke said kindly. "I understand completely."

"You do?"

"Sure. Liberty has a wedding shop in Dallas, as well as one here. I go into town with her from time to time. There's a lot to offer folks in the city. Here in Tulips, we live life at a snail's pace."

"The Gang doesn't seem very snail-like to me," Jessie said. "They seem rather lively."

He grinned. "Be careful. They'd just love to figure out a way to bring you into the fold. Wait until you meet Liberty. Together, they got me to the altar."

She heard the pride in his voice. "I rather like the single life."

"I did, too, for a while. But Liberty had other plans." He laughed. "Actually, that's a small-town big tale. It was hard to catch that little girl, and I did all the chasing."

Jessie smiled as they pulled into the Triple F. "I think I may have heard that from Helen and Pansy."

"You watch those two. If they decide Tulips would be better off with you on the census rolls, here you'll remain. All I do as sheriff is make certain everyone behaves."

Jessie got out of the truck. "Thanks for the ride, Sheriff."

"Sure." He glanced around. "Where's the pink Caddy I've heard so much about?"

"T-bird. Maybe the roadside assistance person moved it."

Zach walked out on the porch, waving. "Good morning."

"Where's her car?" Duke asked.

"I sent it over to Holt's to look at. The roadside repair guy was terrible. Didn't know his hat from his ankle."

"Holt's our town hairdresser," Duke said to Jessie. "It's in good hands now."

Jessie's eyes went wide. "I don't see how hair relates to automobiles."

"Oh, he can fix anything," Duke said easily. "Don't worry about a thing."

Jessie felt her teeth grinding. "Did Holt say how long it would take for him to fix it?"

"No," Zach said. "Come on in and have some breakfast. Pepper's cooking."

"Don't mind if I do," Duke said, striding toward the porch. Jessie hung back.

"Is there a problem?" Zach asked.

"Yes," Jessie said. "I can't seem to get my car back into my possession."

"It's Saturday," Zach said. "What's your hurry?"

Jessie took a deep breath. "I don't trust you. I want away from you, and this town. I feel like I've fallen into Peyton Place, or maybe even Brigadoon, and I want back into the twenty-first century—my life as I know it."

Zach nodded. "You can borrow my truck to get wherever it is you need to go."

Jessie's breath left her for an instant. "Really?"

"Of course." Zach frowned at her. "You're not a prisoner, Jessie. For Pete's sake!"

"I—" She narrowed her eyes.

He shook his head. "You're not being a drama queen, are you?"

Jessie put out her hand. "Keys."

A moment stretched long between them as he

stared at her. Reaching into his pocket, he tugged his keys out and handed them to her.

Jessie looked at him another long moment, clutching the metal pieces of freedom.

"It's over there," he said, pointing. "Happy trails, Jessie."

Chapter Four

Giving Jessie his truck was the fair, manly thing to do. After all, he was hiding her car. This way, he wasn't exactly kidnapping her, as Duke had claimed, threatening to put him in the jail until Jessie left town if he didn't behave. Zach was wisely keeping a bargaining chip. Something precious to her for which she would return. When she came back after the convention, perhaps there would be some light shed on the subject he was most worried about.

He looked at Jessie as she considered his offer, dismayed to realize he was envisioning her in a maternity dress. Liberty could whip Jessie up a beaut.

Shoving that thought from his mind, he shrugged. "The truck's got a full tank of gas. Hit the pedal."

"I don't know," Jessie said. "It seems unfair to take your truck after I hit your livelihood."

"Call me a gentleman," Zach said. "I don't want you in trouble with your boss."

Jessie glanced over at the truck. "My family owns the company. I'm the president of Jessie's Girl Stuff."

He couldn't help smiling. "I sensed you might be a bit of a princess. Tell me more."

"In case I'm the future mother of your child?"

"It's an intriguing thought. I'm not as put off by it as I probably should be, under the circumstances."

"And what are those?" Jessie asked.

"You're a highly excitable female," Zach said. "But I was looking for some excitement so I'm okay with that."

"Funny," she said, "you don't seem like the type to like a high-maintenance woman."

"True. There's a difference between high-maintenance and excitement. I love independence in my women."

"Excellent." Jessie jangled his keys at him and headed toward his truck. "Thanks for the wheels."

"No problem." He headed after her, getting into the passenger seat. "My wheels are your wheels. It's the least I could do for a lady who gave me an afternoon I'll never forget."

She barely glanced at him as she switched on the engine. "Wow. Listen to all that *vroom*."

"Yep," he said happily, putting his arms behind his head. "It's a lot of horses."

"And won't I just look sophisticated when the valet parks my truck at the convention?" She glanced at him. "You can get out now. I've turned on the amazing vehicle without incident."

"Oh, I'm not getting out." Zach grinned at her. "My stuff's all packed and in the truck bed. I like your style of traveling, so I tossed my change of clothes into a hefty bag."

"This hefty bag of mine," she said, holding up her carpetbag, "is a Merada Fine. It cost one thousand, nine hundred and fifty-four dollars. Please do not refer to it in the same breath with a plastic garbage sack, as convenient as one is at times."

"That much money and it doesn't even carry itself. Gosh, you'd think it could run by remote control or something. Or voice activation. 'Purse open,'" he said. "'Purse close.'"

"Very funny. My girlfriend makes these purses, so I'll thank you not to make fun of them. I'm supporting her efforts."

He touched her cheek. "Meradas are actually a respected breed line of horses in Texas. So it's interesting that you're carrying something that's a little less urban than you're used to."

"Coincidence. Nothing more."

He grinned at her stiffness. "We actually have the same sense of humor if you'd ever let yourself smile."

"I smile. Just not around annoying men."

He laughed. "I don't annoy you that badly. Do I?"

"Need you ask?" She backed down the driveway. "I'll take you with me, simply because you're such an excitement freak. This is going to be the most boring thing you've ever done in your life."

"Lots of women there, though." Zach pulled his hat over his face, preparing to snooze while Jessie drove. "As long as my eyeballs are busy and excited, that pretty much takes care of my brain's need for activity."

"It's nice of you to trust me to drive your truck."

"No trust involved. I'm right here, overseeing the whole adventure." Assuaging his conscience from the front seat of his truck was no difficult task, but she didn't know that. Although he tried to drift off, Zach could smell Jessie's fragrance, making it entirely too difficult to relax.

Possibly his senses were overstimulated because he'd been thinking of the upcoming holiday season, which Jessie had mentioned after their glorious afternoon together. He'd always loved winter holidays, most of all when he was a child.

He might have a child one day to decorate the house for, bake for and share stories with. A longing burst inside him that he'd never before recognized. "I never thought I'd want children," he said slowly, and Jessie nodded.

"You've alluded to that."

"If I had kids, though, I'd have a reason to hang candy canes. I like to decorate at the ranch." Zach frowned. "Duke tells me I'm being childish because I love Christmas."

"Didn't you say he's just had a baby? He'll probably beat you to the decorating this year."

Zach grinned, enjoying the thought of the tables turning on his big brother. "I'll be at his elbow every time he puts one raisin on a gingerbread man, every time he hangs an ornament, to tell him how childish he is."

"Probably one reminder of a person's mistakes is enough," Jessie said. "I sure wouldn't want anyone belaboring me over mine."

He raised a brow. "Story time."

"I'm busy driving."

He sent an assessing look her way. "Try one on

me. I know nothing at all about you, except that you have a strong sense of adventure."

"Change has been my downfall. Really."

"Not from my point of view," Zach said sincerely, "unless you count T-bird sex as a pastime."

"I don't," she said, and he grinned.

"Maybe I'm the catalyst for change in your life. I'd count that as being a positive influence."

"Maybe just a pain in the ass," she said, a trace of irritation in her voice.

"Hmm." Zach thought about the sheets of plastic he'd dragged over her pretty T-bird to keep the chickens out of it and decided not to push his luck. No one ever knew what the future would bring. "So did you love him?"

"Who?"

"The ex-boyfriend who cheated on you."

She turned her head to look at him briefly. She'd put on big black sunglasses with gold *G*'s in the corners that made her look like a reclusive movie star, and she had on way too much red lipstick for kissing, although it did look porn-star sexy on her. When they got to know each other better, he was going to tell her that all these girly enticements she was using to subconsciously lure him were not necessary. He liked his women plain and natural.

"I did not," she said. "If I'd loved him, why would I be sitting in a Ford?"

He mulled that. "Perhaps you said Ford in a slightly disdainful tone."

She laughed.

He noticed irritation slipping into his comfort zone. "Fords are the kings of the road, I'll have you know."

There was no response to his allegation. No argument, no comment, *nada.* He rolled his eyes. "If you're going to have my baby, you're going to have to understand a few things."

"I am not having your child," Jessie said. "As much as I wanted a baby, I would not want to make one with you."

Rubbing his chin, he said, "So you're not going to claim your pregnancy is a result of wanting to catch me?"

"I don't think so. And who says I'm pregnant?"

She'd become so saucy. *Snooty,* even.

"I wouldn't even be talking to you right now if you hadn't stolen my car," she said. "Never mind claiming you as the father."

"Aha! You admit it! You wouldn't have told me if I'd given you a baby."

"I would have told you," Jessie said, "but it

wouldn't have mattered to me. I wasn't trying to catch any old guy just to get over my broken heart."

"I thought you said you weren't in love with him."

"Oh." She glanced at him, her lovely eyes hidden by the dark glasses. "My ego was bruised like any normal woman's would be."

"That's code to mean you did love him." Zach thought about that. "So you slept with me on the rebound. Revenge lust."

"Oh, hell no," Jessie said, laughing. "I just—"

He waited, watching the smile slip from her face.

"Well, it's one or the other," he said. "Either you slept with me to subconsciously avenge your boyfriend's treatment of you, or you are, in fact, attracted to me."

"Maybe I was just having a bad-girl moment?"

He rubbed a light finger down her arm. "I don't think so, Jessie T. You're possibly a case, but I also think you're a damn sexy woman who just needs the right man to unlock all your secrets. And I have to warn you—I'm pretty darn good at knowing just how a woman likes her lock picked."

SEVERAL HOURS later it was time to stop for gas. After Zach had bragged about his prowess with women, Jessie turned on the radio and lost herself in her thoughts. Much of what he'd said bothered her—though she would never admit that she'd simply slept with him to avenge herself on her ex. The thought had crossed her mind, of course, but she didn't have to do that to make herself feel better. The simple act of walking away from him had washed away any need for salving her hurt feelings.

The truth was, attraction had surged inside her fast and hot the second she realized Zach had every intention of seducing her. Her answer had been *yes, yes, yes.* The focus of her body had been entirely in the here-now-*more* with Zach.

Her desire for a baby with her ex had been a misplaced sense of emptiness she'd been trying to fill. She knew that and more about herself now. Thanks to the cowboy, she could move past all those feelings of confusion and concentrate on growing as a person and as a woman.

"I don't need change as much as I used to now," she said. "I don't have to beautify everything."

"Yeah, you do," Zach replied, his voice muffled by his hat.

"I was always afraid of letting people down, so I learned to fake everything. I'm never faking again."

"I have to worry about a woman who admits to being a fake. I'd almost worry about our sex life except I know for damn sure you weren't faking anything then."

He didn't have to sound so proud. "You never know. A woman who's had as much practice as I have at faking might be very good at it. Super-convincing."

Grunting, he shoved his hat off his face. "Want me to drive? You've been driving for four hours solid."

"I like driving this beat-up Chevy," Jessie replied, happy to tweak him.

"Jessie, there are certain things I would never do in my life," he began, his voice full of that pompous confidence she had begun to recognize and maybe even admire. "Drive a Chevy is one."

"Really?" she asked, as if she hadn't known he was going to get crazy over her remark.

"Second, I would never let a woman annoy me." Zach took her black sunglasses from her face. "I'm damn tired of not being able to see your big baby blues."

"Give me those."

"Nope," Zach said happily, sticking them inside her carpetbag. "Take you a week to find those now that they're safe inside the loch."

"The loch?"

"A deep, mysterious lake. This purse is symbolic

of the loch in your life. You could hide a baby inside this bag, actually," he said, holding it up with wonder, "and lots of other secrets, which is how you operate your life, I'm betting. You know what, I've had saddlebags smaller than this handbag."

"You're obsessed with my purse."

"But the question is, is it a purse or a suitcase? For the woman who's always prepared to run from the first sight of danger?"

She pursed her lips, fully aware he was probing her for information. "Zach, I'm a simple girl. You're making this too hard."

"How old are you?"

"Twenty-eight."

"Just a baby."

She conducted a mental eye roll or two to allow herself to stay calm. "How old are you, grandpa?"

"Twenty-eight."

She laughed. "And Duke?"

"Thirty. Pepper's twenty-seven. She's the pistol of the family."

"I liked meeting her. She seems very level-headed. And somehow sad."

"Sad? Pepper's not sad. Pepper's the smartest one of the family."

She had definitely picked up on some wistfulness in Pepper's personality. "Zach, while we're at the convention in Los Rios—"

"Which I'm looking forward to, by the way."

"Maybe you could find something to do locally."

"Nah. I know one of the convention speakers and I'm hoping for a front-row seat."

She didn't think that was such a good idea. "There aren't as many women at the conventions as you think there are."

"Oh." He touched her hair. "I had a horse once with hair the color of yours. Very shiny."

"I suppose that's a compliment."

"But you've got all this stiff stuff in your hair today, and your lashes suddenly look like spider legs," he said, drawing near to inspect her. "And there's a lot of red gloss on your lips."

She frowned. "So?"

"So it bugs me. You look like you're hiding the real you. Like you're in costume or something. So is this convention for the grand poobahs of fakers? Because I thought you were giving up on that stuff."

He was in for a big surprise. "Zach, you should call and check on my car."

"I'll do that when we get to the convention. I'm sure I'll have time between seminars."

She shook her head. "You're not going to any seminars."

"I'm not?"

"No," she said, knowing she didn't want Zach that much in her life. There needed to be a fine line between what she did and who she knew. Not every family was homespun like his, not every community was apple-pie sweet. "Here's where you and I part ways." She parked the truck outside the hotel, handed him the key and grabbed her carpetbag. "Happy trails, Zach."

Chapter Five

"Zach decided to accompany Jessie at her convention," Pansy told Helen. "And Pepper just called to tell me that she abandoned him—left him high and dry in Los Rios."

Helen cocked her head. They sat inside the Tulips Saloon, the spot of many a cozy meeting and many a scheme. It was a wonderful second home for the women of the town. They were proud of the tea shop they'd created. Once a lackluster cafeteria with few customers, they'd overridden Duke's objections to calling it a saloon and decided to make a gamble for the tourist trade. "I knew that girl had spunk. I knew she was right for our town the minute I laid eyes on her."

Pansy dusted off the chairs with a tea towel. "She's a bit fancy."

"Zach needs fancy. It will be good for him."
Helen smiled. "Those Forrester kids always liked
whatever was completely opposite from their own
personal experience."

That had been true in Liberty and Duke's case.
Duke was stubborn, and Liberty was…stubborn…
Helen pursed her lips. "Or maybe they like their
own mirror image."

"Then that would make Jessie all wrong." Pansy
got a fresh tea towel and began polishing silver
sleigh-shaped vases. She'd bought pretty red flowers
to go in the vases for color and to spiff up the
ambiance of the Saloon. "There's definitely something going on between those two that is different
from Zach's usual pattern, and I suspect he's interested in her or he wouldn't have gone with her."

"Yes," Helen said thoughtfully. "But if she left
him in Los Rios, what's he going to do now?"

"He's on his way home, according to Pepper.
And not happy about it, either. She said he was all
set to learn about the life of a princess."

"It sounds like there's an edge to those words,"
Helen said. "I found Jessie very down-to- earth."

"Yes," Pansy agreed. "But still, she's definitely
not the type to settle in Tulips, Helen."

Helen frowned, unwilling to concede that point

and yet wondering if her good friend was right. She'd taken a shine to Jessie, she had to admit.

"Remember the goal is to grow Tulips," Pansy said gently. "Duke says it has to be done organically. No bachelor cattle drives."

"Oh, what does Duke know?" Helen had given up on the idea of the bachelor balls when Duke had decided to go along with Zach's idea of building a new elementary school. Zach had wanted to bulldoze the Tulips Saloon, and Duke had saved her precious tearoom from that fate. Zach had gotten his way about the elementary school—a very good idea but Helen only admitted that secretly—and in return, Helen had to give up her schemes for bringing men to Tulips.

But with so many single women in the town, it was hard to grow Tulips without males, and doing it organically might not be possible. Certainly not quick. Zach had dated most of the appropriate females around these parts and none of them had gotten him as far as Houston, much less Los Rios. "We have to work with what we have sometimes, Pansy." She considered her words for a moment. "Do you remember the first rush of being in love?"

Pansy put down her tea towel in surprise. "I remember madness and delight and anticipation."

Helen's cheeks pinked. "So do I. I also re-member that the wonder of love was that it didn't have any rhyme or reason to it."

"Yes," Pansy said, "the emotions were simply there. They existed no matter how much I couldn't believe them or understand them."

"Which would perhaps point to why a woman would leave a handsome man stranded in a strange town."

"Not stranded," Pansy said. "She left him his truck, after all."

"True. We may not have gotten the whole story."

"I'm worried about her car," Pansy admitted. "Something seems fishy about Zach sending Jessie's car to Holt, our lovable hairdresser."

"Holt is wonderful with mechanics. He loves cars! Particularly vintage and special cars. He'll do a wonderful job for Jessie."

"Yes," Pansy said, sinking slowly into a Queen Anne antique chair with cherry blossom design. "Except that Holt never got the car."

Helen blinked. "Holt doesn't have Jessie's T-bird?"

"No." Pansy raised her chin. "I asked him what was wrong with Jessie's car, and he said he didn't have a pink T-bird, nor had he ever met a Jessie.

Nor had Zach called him about fixing any kind of vehicle."

"Oh, my," Helen said. "This is not good."

"I only gently suggest that we mind whom we claim is leaving whom high and dry."

"Point taken. This is a tasty dilemma," Helen said. "Poor Jessie."

Pansy sighed. "I do believe so."

"We're going to need the boys for this one," Helen said, and Pansy nodded.

"As inept as they are, they are the perfect ones to ferret out the male dynamic for us."

"And Jessie's car, to be sure," Helen said. "We must always fortify the position of the female." She reached for the phone. "I will call in the spies, such as they deem themselves."

Pansy smiled. "I love living in Tulips."

BUG CARMINE, self-annointed parade master of Tulips—if they could ever talk Duke into letting them have a parade—and Hiram, who lived in the cell Sheriff Duke presided over by choice, stared at the fancy pink car hidden in one of the Forrester's barns.

"That's some set of wheels," Bug commented. "Mrs. Carmine would like to take a spin in that."

"Looks like a sin-mobile to me," Hiram said.

"In my day, girls that drove something like that would have been the ones you wouldn't take home to Mother."

"Yeah." Bug placed the cover carefully over it again. "Now that we've found it, we have to make a decision. Either we tell the ladies it's here and they bust Zach, or we say we didn't find it, and let matters really get hot in Tulips."

"Can't put 'Here Lives A Car Thief' on a town billboard." Hiram shook his head. "Still, I like the idea of putting one over on the TSG. What crime has Zach committed anyway? It's good that he likes a girl enough to steal her car."

Bug sniffed. "In my day, we sent flowers as a token of our affection."

"These are different times," Hiram said, "as you should know from what the Tulips Saloon Gang regularly put us through."

"There is that," Bug agreed. "We can't tell on Zach. Bringing the TSG down on his head—well, I couldn't stand to see that happen to him."

"Yeah, they're still mad at him for his idea to bulldoze the saloon and make an elementary school out of it." They walked out of the barn and closed the door. "As far as I'm concerned, I never saw a thing," Hiram said.

"Nor me." Bug shook his friend's hand.

"My conscience is clear," Hiram said with satisfaction as they walked away. "I do love keeping secrets from the gals, and tonight, I'll sleep like a baby with my conscience for a blanket."

TO ZACH'S SURPRISE, days passed without any word from Jessie. When the weeks slipped into December and he still hadn't heard a word from her about her beloved car, he knew he had a big problem on his hands.

A tulip-pink convertible land yacht wasn't easy to hide. It was only a matter of time before Duke or Pepper went into that outlying barn for something. Duke was busy with Liberty and the new baby, and Pepper was busy doing whatever she was doing, but time wouldn't be on Zach's side forever.

He couldn't believe Jessie hadn't returned for her car. He'd thought he was being so smart, so in control of the situation.

Of course, he should have known better when Jessie asked the convention security to have him blocked from the site under the guise of it being for women only, a trick she had eerily in common with Pansy and Helen and the other TSG members. He'd hung around until the convention was over but he'd never caught another glimpse of Jessie. The people at the checkout desk had been supremely unhelpful, but he'd finally bribed a young clerk into telling him that the entire mascara-and-lipstick crowd was long gone. The president, the clerk had told him in a whisper, had left by helicopter.

No wonder he hadn't seen Jessie escape. He'd only been patrolling the glass-and-brass hotel doors, not the rooftop.

Maybe she'd never return and he'd have a lifetime souvenir of the one golden afternoon they'd shared. He'd forever remember how he'd worried that she'd give him a child, and she'd given him a vehicle instead. Not to mention that it was a completely inappropriate ride for him to be seen driving, so she'd cornered him in a lose-lose situation that would do nothing except color his reputation pink or get him in deep brown with Duke.

"Okay, you win," he muttered under his breath. "Just come get your damn car before Duke finds it."

JESSIE LOVED spending the weeks leading up to the holidays on the road. Her job was glamorous and fun. She loved to travel. Meeting people and helping women to look their best was her favorite part of the job, especially at this time of the year. This was her moment to help ladies shine, like ornaments that stayed in storage all year and came out radiant for the holiday season.

Hopefully, what she taught them stayed with them the rest of the year, too. That hope of helping women was what she'd built her position on at her company, and was the driving factor behind its success today.

Hot pink was the color of her life.

Her parents had known that when they'd chosen her car, her promotion gift. No mere heiress's job, her father had said that her vision held the direction the company needed.

She looked at her best friend as they sat in the living room of her suite at the world-class hotel her parents owned. Fran Carter was also her secretary and together the two of them had cooked up this year's special holiday look. It had almost been glittering and fabulous enough to keep her mind off a certain cowboy, but Jessie hadn't forgotten him despite the miles she'd put between them.

It would be impossible to forget Zach.

"So, Jessie T.," Fran said, curling up on a coffee-colored suede sofa, "we know all about how to cry so your mascara won't run and your fakies won't fall off, and how to make things look a helluva lot prettier than they really are. But I don't know a makeup trick for what you need."

Jessie shook her head. "The thing is," Jessie said slowly, "I think I would have fallen for Zach no matter what. He was pretty smooth for a man who grew up far away from sophisticated surroundings."

Fran nodded. "You could call him."

"I really can't," Jessie said. "If I do, he'll think I'm just looking for my car."

"It *was* a helluva calling card you left him," Fran said. "Eventually, he'd understand that your call wasn't completely about your vehicle."

"I'd never met anyone as stubborn as Zach. I'm afraid I didn't exercise good judgment in leaving him behind. My feet seemed to take flight of their own accord." No man had ever made her feel that nervous before, and escape had seemed the logical and only action.

"You've always put your job first," Fran said. "Don't be so hard on yourself. So you had a fling. It's completely understandable." She giggled. "Although out of character, I'll admit."

Jessie looked out the window at the skyline of the city. It was beautiful in Dallas, and she loved living here. But… "This is not where I want to raise a child," she said quietly.

"I know," Fran said. "Which is the real reason he'll know you calling is not about the car."

"His worst nightmare," Jessie murmured. "He told me so more than once."

Fran nodded. "We all have nightmares eventually."

Jessie touched her stomach. His nightmare was actually her dream come true.

At least part of her dream.

Chapter Six

It was a cold December this year, with gray twilight skies leading into dark nights. Zach hung candy canes on the Christmas tree in the Forrester living room rather morosely, thinking that Duke's child was too young to appreciate the decorations, and nobody but him seemed to carry on the holiday spirit.

Only this year, his holiday spirit had been flagging. Even a visit from the ghost of Christmases past would have livened things up a bit for him.

The ghost he'd least expected to appear got out of a yellow taxi and turned toward the house, catching him gawking out the window at her. His breath completely left him as Jessie waved hello.

She's come to get her car, Zach thought, squashing the relief rushing through him that Jessie had returned to Tulips. The doorbell rang. Zach dashed a hand through his hair, wished he was clean-shaven and decided he didn't care what had brought her back. He just thanked his lucky Christmas stars he was going to get to lay eyes on her one more time.

She'd scared him by leaving his pink ransom-mobile so long without even a call to check up on it.

He jerked open the door.

She looked at him silently.

"Do I know you?" he asked, trying to be funny. So many emotions rushed through him that he lost his place in his be-cool script.

"In the biblical sense," Jessie said, strolling into his living room. "Neither of us knows each other in any other sense, of course."

He'd forgotten how his wit never disarmed her—she could come right back with her own zinger. "I'm surprised you could find your way back here without a trail of bread crumbs or something."

She pulled a checked cashmere scarf from her neck. "The taxi driver didn't have any trouble finding the Forrester ranch."

She wouldn't even admit that she knew exactly where he lived—er, where her car was. He narrowed his gaze on her. "Make yourself at home, I guess, since you're here."

"Thank you." Sitting gingerly across from the tree, she studied his efforts. "Just getting started?"

He'd been at this chore all afternoon. "Yes. I suppose your tree is up and looks like Mrs. Claus decorated it personally."

Jessie blinked. "I never did ask you how Brahma Bud was. I hope he didn't suffer any effects from hitting my car."

Zach crossed his arms, taking in the delicate bones of her face and the gentle lines of her features. "*You* hit *him,* as I recall. He was minding his own business, entirely unaware that females driving pink cars might be bad for his health."

"So he's fine."

Zach sighed. "Yes. Thank you for asking."

She nodded. "I was worried about him."

"So worried that you called. Say, did you know that some people actually leave a building by helicopter when they're avoiding someone?"

Jessie stood. "I've come at a bad time. If I could just have my car keys—"

"Certainly." Reaching into a cabinet in the living room, he pulled out the keys and handed them to her. "And now that you have what you want, let me show you to your car. I think you'll find that it's been kept in the very best possible condition."

"Zach—"

He turned. "The car is this way. I'll drive you to the barn. I'm sure your schedule doesn't allow you much time to sit and chat."

She looked at him for a long moment. "No. It doesn't," she finally said. "And I'd like to pay a visit to the ladies before it gets any later."

He raised a brow, surprised. "Pansy and Helen?"

"Well, yes," Jessie said. "I don't expect to be coming this way again, and I'd like to say hello."

Of course she wouldn't come through Tulips again. His heart began a restless pounding as he considered his options, which appeared few and unfortunate. As in none. He couldn't keep her here: he'd already tried that and she'd shown a remarkable ability to outwit him. He'd tried romance, but she hadn't been exactly banging down his bedroom door to throw herself into his den of sexual pleasure again. *A normal woman would,* he told himself sourly, just to keep his pride from ebbing away. "Are you hungry?" he asked suddenly. The silence had stretched long, he was out of options and blurting anything, even the offer of a hamburger, was his brain's desperate appeal to keep her with him another moment or two.

"I am," she said solemnly. "Are you?"

If she was hungry, he was hungry. Whatever it took. "Ravenous," he said. "I could eat a horse. And the barn."

Jessie looked at him. "I seem to be eating more lately."

Her eyes widened. He glanced down the length of her body, admiring her pretty red coat, her winter boots and pantsuit of some soft fabric which went well with her whiskey-colored hair. "You look great to me," he said. "If you're eating more, it's certainly going in the right places." Her breasts looked great, he thought. Her figure was curvaceous, perhaps a bit curvier than he remembered, but heck, at the time he hadn't been paying as much attention to the form as the opportunity to…his gaze shot to hers. "Everybody seems to eat more during the holidays."

She nodded slowly, her eyes holding his.

His heart began to beat hard in his chest, nearly stealing his breath, almost painfully choking it from him. "You wouldn't be trying to tell me in your refined way that you're…eating more because you're eating for two, would you?" he asked, his whole body tensing as he watched her eyes.

Her gaze dropped for just an instant, but in that instant he knew that he had followed in his brother

Duke's footsteps. "I'll be damned," he murmured, trying to sort out how he felt. Delighted, devastated, shocked, scared—

"Actually, three," she said quietly, her eyes moving back to catch his.

He blinked. "Three what?"

She shrugged. "I'm eating for three. Me, and the twins. Merry Christmas, Zach."

JESSIE WATCHED as Zach sat heavily, his gaze locked on hers. Helplessness washed over her.

"So much for your method," he said. "I could have said no, I could have worn a raincoat, but I fell for you like a starving man for food."

She walked out the front door, keys in hand.

Catching her hand, he turned her toward him. "What's your hurry? Looks like we're going to be spending a lifetime together, City."

"It's so annoying when you call me that," she snapped, wishing she felt more relieved now that he knew but only feeling guilt. "My name is Jessie."

"And a wonderful name it is, gorgeous." He kissed her on the lips, surprising her so much she didn't pull away. "We'll be naming the twins together."

She hadn't thought that far ahead. Names had not been high on her list of priorities—figuring out how to tell Zach had been first. "You could take one, and I'll take the other."

"Nah." He gave her stomach a mischievous eyeing. "Two? How are they both going to fit in that little tiny tummy? Two of my big, strapping sons?" He put a hand on her still-flat stomach. "If they're anything like Duke and me, they're going to be fighting for space constantly."

"This topic just doesn't feel as light to me as it seems to be for you," she said. "I'm still trying to make sense of it. Just the stress of having to tell you—"

The last two weeks of planning, worrying and stalling had finally worn her down. Tears burst out of nowhere, running down her face before she could compose herself.

"Uh-oh," Zach said. "That's the main difference between pregnant women and pregnant cows, I guess. Emotions."

She wiped at her face quickly. "I could tell you were a sensitive male the first time I met you."

He wiped her tears away with his thumbs. "You're cute when you spring a leak."

Jessie moved away from him. "Could you direct me to my car, please?"

"I could, but you'll probably tell me a few more

things you're keeping from me. You're kind of like a firecracker that way. If I wait long enough, information just explodes—"

"Zach," she said, "are you in shock?"

"Yes."

She sighed. "I thought so. I've been a bundle of nerves because I knew how mad you'd be."

"Well, I am mad," he said, "but I'm not going to be upset in front of the children."

"The children?"

"Yes." He put a protective hand on her stomach. "They need to know from day one that they're loved, anticipated and cherished. Our family is very close, in our own oddly special way."

She looked at him. "So the reason you're acting so nonchalant is that you're faking it for the children?"

"Faking it doesn't sound right." He touched her carefully constructed eyelashes. "From now on, I don't want you wearing any more of this goo around me."

"I make my living with this goo," she said, and he nodded.

"I make my living with bulls and things, but I'm not going to make you look at them all the time. I prefer natural skin on my woman."

"Zach, I am not your woman. I will never be your woman," Jessie said. "I don't even know you."

"That's going to be a problem," Zach said, "since I am your prince charming. Your knight in shining armor."

"I don't need the platitudes of fairy tales," she said hotly, making Zach laugh.

"Okay, we're stuck with each other for life," he said. "How's that for relationship lingo? When we're at the boys' soccer matches, we'll introduce each other as 'this is the person I'm stuck with forever.' People won't talk, I'm sure. Not in Tulips."

He wasn't going to make her life easy. Racing ahead into the future, thoughts of Zach made her brain whirl. Ever since the thin blue line had shown up on her pregnancy test, and the super-shocking news of a double pregnancy had been confirmed by her doctor, Jessie had been holding her breath. Trying to think how to tell a man she barely knew that he was going to be a father. She hadn't thought of baby names, nor soccer games, nor what the two of them would be to each other. She'd dreaded having to tell him, but since she knew his worst fear—that he'd be a father and his children would never know him—she wanted him to know as fast as she could tell him. Dealing with all the other consequences she'd put on the back burner.

He had the pot on the front burner, turned to full boil. Strangely, he didn't seem to mind the heat. "I thought you'd be scary about this."

"I'm going to be scary in a little while," Zach said easily. "When I have to tell Pansy and Helen, I'll probably be at my worst. They're going to be so pleased." He gave her a wry glance. "My brother the sheriff says he wants the town to grow organically, which is not quite what the Gang wants. They're going to love the fact that they're getting two little organic sprouts out of one Forrester. They'll say it serves me right, and then smile into their fragile little teacups."

"I don't understand."

He shook his head. "Just be prepared for the Gang to give you a very large baby shower."

"I don't want that," Jessie said quickly. "Can't we come to an agreement about this?"

A frown crossed his face. He stared down at her, his brows knit tightly together. "Agreement?"

She swallowed. "Um, a custody agreement?"

"No," he said, his gaze like dark glass, "and never talk like that in front of the children again. Ever."

ZACH WAS MORE SURPRISED than he let on to Jessie about his impending fatherhood. But he wasn't surprised this was happening. The moment he'd seen her, he'd known she would change his life—and she had.

They didn't even know each other, and what he did know about her signaled a bumpy road ahead. She was flighty. He was methodical. She was spoiled. He was hardworking.

Those differences were just the beginning. He looked at her, imagining her with a big, round belly, and wanted to rub his hands with glee. Twins! It was a Christmas miracle as far as he was concerned, and he wanted this new phase in their relationship to start well. He wasn't saying one thing to upset her. "Were you planning on telling Helen and Pansy? Is that why you really wanted to go into town?"

"I…don't know." She put her keys into her purse and sat back down. "I know I was planning on telling you. That's all I knew."

"So you're moving out here with me," he said, leaning against a wall, quickly trying to devise a plan. "Or I'm moving somewhere with you."

"No," Jessie said. "We're not moving anywhere, at least not together."

He frowned at her. "Look. We're not throwing

away what we did as just an afternoon of freebie sex. We need to become closer."

She appeared to shrink into her coat. "I don't understand you. I know that this is your worst fear come true."

"Yeah." He scratched under his hat. "Funny how it doesn't seem that bad now that it's happened. If that was my life's biggest fear, maybe I never had anything to be really afraid of."

She smiled. "You're not going to say that I tried to trap you?"

"Did you?"

"No!"

He laughed. "Oh, come on. Leave a guy with a little ego."

She stood. "I'm not interested in your ego. I would never cling to a man, or trap him, or—"

"Jessie," he said softly, reaching for her hand to calm her down, "when I met you, you were hot-footing it away from a boyfriend or ex-fiancé or husband or something. You're clearly not the kind of woman who lets men influence her life. I know you're a big shot in your company and that you're more likely to wear pants than panty hose. I get it, okay? Don't keep worrying that I think you're some thimble-brained woman who can't take care of herself."

"Thimble-brained?"

"Those things Pansy and Helen are always using to sew with and stuff."

She nodded. "Nice analogy."

He gave her a wry look. "I know you're not ready to walk down the aisle with me. You can relax. The electric fence you've got up around you is shooting sparks at me."

She sighed. "I don't mean to be so uneasy."

"Well, don't get too comfortable, either," Zach said, grinning. "I don't want to be taken for granted now that you've gotten what you wanted from me."

"Zach!"

He crossed his boots and stared at her. "You did say you had planned to get pregnant as soon as possible after the wedding."

"Yes, but my fiancé was not a stranger." She gave him a haughty look. "Wanting children is not unusual inside a marriage."

He shrugged. "I should hire myself out for stud. I have bulls that don't perform so successfully."

She rolled her eyes. "I'm leaving to tell Pansy and Helen. I need female advice. Yours isn't worth a damn."

"That's what I hear," he said cheerfully. "It comes from being middle child."

"Whatever," she said.

"I'll drive you if you promise not to steal my truck."

"You have no worries," she said, and he nodded.

"Good. We can break the news together. First we have to tell Duke, of course. Pepper we can tell by phone because we hardly see her anymore."

Jessie backed up a step. "You can tell your brother by yourself."

He grinned, liking that she was feeling a little bit nervous. It made him feel big and strong and protective. "Duke won't throw you in jail."

She stiffened. "Of course not! What charges would he have?"

"You were trespassing," he reminded her.

"I was lost," she snapped.

"You did assault my livelihood with a deadly weapon. Poor Brahma Bud."

She sniffed. "Any other charges?"

"You did steal my heart," he said, trying to be light but realizing the moment he said it that he'd made a serious error. Jessie's eyes went dark.

"I stole nothing worth keeping, then," she said. "Consider it returned."

"Whew, prickly," he said. "Did you know you have a habit of being prickly when you're nervous?"

She stared up at him, her gaze very serious. "Did you know you have a habit of trying to be funny when you're nervous? It doesn't go over very well."

"Why would I be nervous?"

"Impending fatherhood, a woman you only met once, your worst fears realized, telling your brother—" She paused. "I can't decide which of those nerves of yours is most rattled."

"You may have a point." He rubbed his chin. "I don't know how to act. Mainly, I don't want you to go away before I get to know you better. That's my biggest worry now."

He meant it, even if sounded silly. How could he do the right thing for her, and for his children, unless he knew who Jessie Farnsworth really was?

"These kids of mine are going to matter to me a lot," he said gruffly. "I know you've got a busy life, but...marry me, Jessie."

Chapter Seven

An offer of marriage from Zach was the last thing Jessica had expected from him. Her heart took a dizzying leap. *If only it were that easy.*

"I know you're not the marrying kind," he said, "but we could probably work out a satisfactory arrangement."

She blinked. "Arrangement?"

"Yeah. I don't know what. But something we could both live with."

The front door opened, and they moved away from each other. Duke walked in, sleet spilling off his hat. "Howdy," he said to Zach. "Well, hello, Jessie."

"Hi, Duke," she said, sending a worried glance Zach's way. Her composure had deserted her with the marriage proposal. Surely he hadn't been serious!

Yet a secret part of her wondered what marriage to Zach might be like.

"Hope I'm not interrupting anything," Duke said. "Liberty says she needs some bolts of plastic covering she stored in one of the barns. I'm not sure which one. Hellish weather to search four barns but at least you made it in before the storm, Jessie. I heard the roads were freezing up just east and north of Tulips. It's on its way here."

Zach frowned. "Plastic covering?"

"Yeah. There should be several rolls of it. Big enough to cover the carpet in a wedding chapel."

"I never saw bolts of plastic," Zach said.

"You don't go into all the barns regularly," Duke said. "Jessie, you look well. Are you in for a couple of days?"

She shook her head. "I wasn't planning on it."

Duke looked from Jessie to Zach. "Well, good to see you all the same. I'm off to root around out there."

"No!" Zach crammed a hat on his head and pulled his keys from his pocket. "I'll look. You stay here and keep Jessie company."

Duke looked bemused. "I don't think I should do that, Zach. I believe she came to see you."

Zach nodded. "That's true. So I'll just head off now and do that looking around for you. I'll call you if I find any of the plastic. In the meantime, grab some soup off the stove and try to warm up."

Duke looked at him. "Hell, Zach, you wouldn't have even known I was at the ranch if I hadn't walked in. Just pretend like you don't know I'm on the property and go on doing what you were doing." Duke turned to leave. "You're acting nuttier than a Christmas fruitcake, which, by the way, the ladies whipped up for us. Full of pecans and things. Be sure to stop by my office and have a bite, Jessie. The Gang can cook for certain, and this is the time of year when they really get their aprons on. Our neighboring-town baker, Valentine, has challenged them to a poppyseed cake bake-off, and that's a holiday snack I look forward to."

Zach slid out the door while his brother was completing his polite goodbye to her. Jessie looked at Zach's retreating back, surprised. "He definitely doesn't want you to get chilled," she told Duke.

"He is one strange apple that fell off our family tree. If I didn't know better, I'd think there was something in one of the barns he didn't want me to see."

"Oh," Jessie said. "I thought strange was his normal behavior."

"I can see why you'd think that." Duke sighed. "Come on. I can't leave you here alone, though my brother has no manners. You can sit in my nice warm truck while we search. Who would want to get married the first week in December, anyway?" he grumbled, holding Jessie's elbow as she walked so she wouldn't slip.

Jessie shook her head. "Liberty's brave to handle gowns and wedding details. I'd be too worried to have brides as my clientele."

They got in Duke's truck. "Zach says you do makeup for conventions of women. That sounds just as challenging as brides. Women in search of beauty would terrify me."

Jessie smiled. "Female dreams aren't scary. Really, they're not. Females want what males want."

"I've only been married a couple of months and haven't figured that out yet," Duke said with a chuckle. "What the hell?" Stopping the truck, he shone the brights into the barn, which Zach had obviously reached at a breakneck speed.

Jessie squinted into the darkness. "Looks like a whole lot of plastic wrap covering something big." She got out of the truck and followed Duke.

Zach was busily tucking the plastic onto a large roll, while diligently keeping his back to whatever object he was removing the plastic from.

"What the hell?" Duke asked. "You didn't use Liberty's wedding aisle-covering stuff, did you, Zach?"

"Quite by accident," Zach said. "You two go on back to the house and get warm. I'll be done in a jif and bring this plastic with me."

"Yeah, but what the hell you used it for is what I want to know," Duke said, approaching Zach. But Jessie already knew.

"My car!" she said. "You jerk, you never got it repaired." Anger flooded her. "Which means it was never broken in the first place."

"Well," Zach said, and he would have said more, but Jessie turned away so she wouldn't slap the excuse right out of his mouth before he could tell her any more lies.

She got into Duke's truck without saying a word. Duke also got in, leaving the plastic wrap behind, and silently started the engine. Unable to stop herself, Jessie peeked at Zach. He stood forlornly in front of her car, which was still half-covered with wrap. Sleet began pelting the roof of the truck and bounced off the barn roof.

"Storm's coming in," Duke said gently. "I'm sure not making excuses for my brother, but you don't want to drive that pretty car in this weather, anyway. It's not good for a convertible."

She was too mad—and too hurt—to speak.

Duke sighed. "I'll drive you into Pansy's. One of the old gals would just love to put you up for the night. Or longer. They'll pamper you thoroughly."

She nodded. He turned the truck around, leaving Zach.

"I'd like to say something good about my kid brother—"

"You should arrest that car thief, Sheriff." The words came out a whole lot more bitter than she wanted them to sound.

"I never considered that," Duke said. "You have a point. But you don't really want him locked up, do you?"

She sighed. "He'd just get on your nerves while you tried to work."

"Are you sure you don't know my brother very well?"

Well enough to be having children with him. "Better than I'd like to, at this point."

"When the weather clears and it's safe for you

to drive out from the ranch, I'll make certain Zach gets your car to you, in complete working order."

"Thank you."

"I have to be honest, I'm a bit surprised by my brother's behavior. Though I'm trying not to rush to judgment, I'd like to apologize on behalf of the Forrester family for my brother's prank. I really am surprised by him."

Duke would be more surprised if he knew he was going to be an uncle.

He pulled into a driveway. "But these three houses are friendly territory. Miss Pansy's, Miss Helen's and then Liberty's house, which she's also converted into a wedding shop. We still stay here when we need to be closer to town, though. When bad weather comes in, I like being near my office. I can walk from here."

The houses were small and quaint, certainly not like anything Jessie had ever lived in. "Are you sure I won't be putting anyone out?"

"The ladies will be delighted to have company. I promise." He waved to them as they came out on their respective porches, and Jessie smiled, delighted to see the ladies again. Duke came around to her door just as Zach's truck pulled up behind them in the driveway. He got out, slamming his door.

"I can take over from here, Duke," Zach said.

"I don't think so," Duke said with a scowl. "You have a lot of explaining to do, and I don't know that you're operating honestly where this woman is concerned."

"I'm trying to marry her," Zach said.

"That might have nothing to do with honesty on your part," Duke snapped, but Jessie's eyes widened. Pansy clasped her hands together, and Helen's mouth puckered.

"That's no proposal," Helen said, coming forward to shoo Jessie toward her house. "Pansy, be careful coming down those steps. Come on over and I'll make us some tea. It's so good to see you again, Jessie. We wondered when you'd return."

"Yes," Pansy said, giving her a hug. "When is the baby due?"

Duke stared at her, surreptitiously shooting a glance at her midsection, which was concealed by her red wool coat. "Baby?"

"How did you know?" Jessie asked Pansy.

"You glow, my dear. You simply glow. And you've put on a teensy bit of very flattering weight."

Duke put his hands on his hips. "Is that why you stole her car?"

Helen gasped. "Stole her car?"

"Yes. It's hidden in one of our barns."

Pansy gave Zach's arm a light slap. "Shame on you, Zach. Your parents would be so disappointed."

Zach sighed. "You people are not helping."

"I bet those rascals found the car and never told us," Helen said to Pansy. "I'm going to give them what-for when I see them."

Pansy nodded. "Jessie, we sent out a search team to check on your vehicle. But they failed us." She gave a haughty sniff at Zach. "You can't hijack a lady when you want to get to know her better, even if she's having your child."

"Children," Zach said.

"Children?" Duke repeated, glowering at his brother.

"We're having twins," Jessie said.

Duke grinned. "Way to go, Bro! Nice shooting!"

The women groaned. "Come on, Pansy," Helen said. "We've had enough excitement for the night, and Jessie needs her rest."

Pansy wiped the delighted grin from her face so she could level a stern look at Zach. "And no climbing through windows or any other shenanigans to talk to Jessie. She'll talk to you when we're good and ready. You just go cool your heels, Zach."

Jessie was fine with that. She was stunned to find that Zach had lied to her. "Thank you for the ride, Duke," she said, allowing Pansy and Helen to lead her away.

"Hey! How about my marriage proposal?" Zach asked.

"We never heard one," Helen called over her shoulder as they walked away. "We heard a stubborn man trying to get his way with little effort, though."

"Thank you," Jessie said as the door closed behind them. It was nice to be out of the cold, and even better to be inside the welcoming doors of Helen's cozy house. "The only bright spot in this is that when Liberty finds out Zach used her precious wedding floor covering to protect my car, she's going to be annoyed. I don't know that it can be used now for the purposes for which it was intended."

"It'll be good for Zach to have a bunch of females peeved with him," Pansy said, taking Jessie's coat. "Hopefully, it'll smarten him up."

"That's for certain." Helen set the kettle on the stove. "He's been quite spoiled since we have so few males in town. So few reasonably intelligent males."

Pansy giggled. "So much for our spies. They're either terrible at their job, or conspiring against us."

Jessie looked at the women. "Why would your friends not tell you if they knew my car was perfectly fine?"

"To be on the boys' side," Helen said simply. "This town has always been about the battle of the sexes. And we girls always win."

Pansy giggled as the three of them sat at the table together. A pretty lamp with a cut-out shade sent warm light around the kitchen. Jessie relaxed, feeling like she was home for the very first time in her life.

Chapter Eight

Zach cooled his heels for as long as he could stand it—approximately ten hours—and despite the bad weather, drove over to Helen's. He just had to see Jessie. Okay, she'd shocked the hell out of him. He hadn't reacted appropriately—heaven only knew he hadn't done *anything* appropriately.

But there was a lot of history in his life that forced him to seek appropriate action where Jessie and his kids were concerned. He'd had a major Christmas present tossed at him, and he was determined to learn how to keep it.

Fortunately for him, he was a Forrester, and so far, the Forrester family was one-for-one on figuring out when to keep their hands on their pregnant significant other.

Pepper would be too smart to let herself get

ahead of the romance, he thought sourly. Younger sisters shouldn't be so calm, cool and collected about everything—only the men in the family seemed to have a hard time with relationships.

"It should be the other way around," he muttered, thinking about last night's impromptu proposal which had brought him no credit whatsoever with Jessie, Duke or the Gang, either, for that matter. As much as they adored hearing about proposals, they'd barely paid his any attention.

They hadn't taken him seriously—which seemed to be a theme in his life. He stared at Helen's house, wondering how to approach the puzzle his world had become. Should he try romance?

"Little late for that." Jessie wouldn't take him seriously on the romance issue. He had to be very careful with his pursuit because she possessed a natural-born wanderer's foot. She could take off any time, in any method of transportation, and it might be months before he laid eyes on her again.

Perhaps help was required in this matter. He pulled out his phone and dialed Holt, investor and civic-minded counterpart to the Gang. Holt sided with the ladies, but he also sided with the men sometimes, and was guaranteed to give a rational and unbiased opinion.

"Holt," he said when he heard a brisk hello on the other end of the line.

"Yes, Zach," Holt said. "I already know why you're calling. I heard your little lady is back in town wanting her car, and that you told her I was supposedly fixing it. I don't like being in the middle if I don't know what's going on."

Great. Life wasn't good when the only hairdresser in town was in a tizzy with him. "Sorry about that. It seemed like a good excuse at the time."

"It didn't work, though, did it?"

"No," Zach said, sighing.

"So now she's returned, and she wants her car, and you want some visitation. That's what I hear through the grapevine," Holt said.

"Grapevine's right," Zach replied. "I want custody of my kids if Jessie won't marry me."

Holt sighed. "The only way you can achieve that is through the courts, Zach."

"I was thinking flowers, maybe some time alone together—"

"You called for my opinion," Holt said. "Becoming a father with a woman whom you've greatly aggravated is not a position of equanimity, you know."

He wasn't sure what equanimity was, but it

didn't sound like he was in a good place with Jessie. "But if you met her—"

"I did." Holt sniffed. "Not that you brought her by. Helen invited me to come meet the newest Tulips citizen."

Zach frowned. "I doubt you'll ever be able to call Jessie a citizen of Tulips."

"At the rate you're going, no."

Everybody is a critic. Zach said, "Do you have any advice, or are you just going to ride the Zach's-A-Louse bandwagon?"

"Legal documentation. And remember she has two legal eagle brothers. The deck may be pretty well stacked in her favor."

"Legal eagle brothers?" Zach listened to the dial tone in his ear. "That was so helpful."

Drumming his fingers on the steering wheel, he looked at the three small, two-story houses that so delicately hid the strength residing within them. Jessie did fit in with that group of strong women, he realized. He had been attracted to her strength from the moment he'd met her. She wasn't the kind of woman who flirted. She didn't put on airs around a man. With Jessie, he'd learned that what he saw was pretty much what he got, straightforward and honest.

That was some small comfort, but he couldn't help mulling the rebound factor. She'd been in a vulnerable time in her life when they'd met.

He conceded that he might have come across as a bit ham-handed and perhaps even a bit horny. Those might be reasons she hadn't taken his marriage proposal seriously.

"Like I just jump on every cute girl I meet." He stared at Helen's house through slivers of sleet bouncing off his windshield. He owed it to his children—and he and Jessie—to present himself and his plan one more time, even if he had to do it in Miss Helen's living room.

He got out of the truck and went to the door. On the door hung a piece of paper that read, "At Liberty's." He went to the middle house and rang the doorbell. Duke answered, shaking his head at his brother. "Next door," he said, while Molly-Jimbo barked a welcome at Zach. Duke closed the door. Zach headed to the final house, finding the front door open and about ten women standing in the entryway of Miss Pansy's.

"Did I miss a party?" he asked, wondering how he could have missed seeing the parked cars or commotion or something.

The ladies went quiet. In front of the fireplace

sat Jessie. At her feet were small gifts of welcome, ranging from knitted baby booties to decorated cloth baby diapers. There was even a stack of recipe cards.

Pansy came over to give him a hug. "We're having a very tiny, most last-minute welcoming party. Holt's been by as well."

"I heard," Zach said, not feeling too happy that he was left out of the fun.

"Well, it's a wonderful day for hot tea and cookies," Pansy said. "And who knows when we might get another chance to introduce Jessie to some of the girls? Thankfully your brother didn't mind rounding everybody up in his truck and bringing them over. It couldn't have been more fun if it was a sleighing party! Duke even wore a Santa hat."

Jessie watched him, her eyes wide and somewhat worried. Since some of the "girls" were between sixty and eighty years of age, Zach realized his audience was one of romantic souls.

He decided to play to that audience. "Hi, Jessie."

"Hi." She barely glanced at him.

Whew. Frosty as the cold air outside. "Hope you'll forgive me about the car," he said. "I got carried away."

A murmur went around the room.

"You certainly did," Jessie said.

"Though I kept your car in excellent shape," he said.

"Yes," Liberty said. "You owe me for plastic—"

"I certainly do," Zach said quickly, before the subject could move from his intentions to his sins. "Jessie, I know I asked you to marry me too quickly—"

The murmur went around the room again, this time with more excitement. Jessie watched him, her gaze suspicious.

"But I want you to know I'm willing to wait," Zach continued, "a long time, if I have to, to get your 'yes.'"

The ladies turned to look at Jessie, whose cheeks had gone strawberry-pink.

"Thank you," Jessie replied, "but my answer must remain no. You lied to me, Zach Forrester, and I'd never be able to trust you. Plus, it was a silly scheme, if you ask me. I should send you a bill for all the travel inconvenience you've caused me."

This wasn't going to be easy. "I'd pay that bill and any other," Zach said. "You could have come to get your car anytime. Why didn't you?"

The audience turned to look at her again. Jessie shifted on her chair. "I didn't want to see you again."

The room went so silent a teacup could have cracked and no one would have noticed.

"By the time Thanksgiving passed, I realized I was expecting," she said, lifting her chin. "I decided this was something I needed to do myself. Of course, at the time, I thought something was terribly wrong with my car and you were honestly trying to get it repaired. I had no idea you'd simply hijacked it."

The ladies leveled frowns on him.

Miss Helen stood. "Well, I must say, perhaps this isn't the time or place for this discussion," she said gently. "But all the same, Jessie, I must speak on behalf of Zach."

Zach blinked. Was one of the town's most sturdy pillars going to put in a good word for him?

"Zach has ever been the more impulsive Forrester," Helen said, with Pansy nodding in agreement. "And yet, he has a heart of gold so that one must love him in spite of his foibles."

Jessie looked surprised to hear that, as was Zach himself. *Go on. Now we're getting somewhere,* he thought gratefully. He wanted to be loved in spite of whatever that thing was she said he had.

"His brother spent a great deal of time trying to

derail our best plans," Helen said, "but Liberty's tamed him now so there's very little chance of that."

The ladies laughed. Jessie shifted again, not meeting Zach's eyes.

"Pepper is her own woman. Very independent, much more so than her brothers."

"Hey," Zach said, "can Duke and I vote on that?"

"It's true and you know it," Pansy said. "If you'd but admit it. She went off and got a medical degree. She is trying to grow the town with the clinic she wants to start."

"Well," Helen said, "Duke's idea of growing the town is to just hope and pray the sky rains interested newcomers who want to settle a fair piece from city life."

"He's becoming more broad-minded," Liberty said.

"Only because you have a shop in the city as well as here," Helen said. "He's learned to admit that there must be something that draws people to a place. We had no railroad and we're no port city. Big industrial farms have changed the livelihoods for many of us. We missed some opportunities to show that our light could shine brightly," Helen said. "But along comes Zach, and he disagrees with his brother, and has a big idea."

Zach nodded, liking the way Helen was making him look smart and important, all very necessary to be the man he thought Jessie might want. She began packing the welcome gifts into a sack, looking at him askance.

"I'm starting to see a theme here."

"What?" Zach asked.

"Good ideas, wrong follow-through," she said.

"Possibly," he said, "though I really believe my ideas are just bigger in scope than other people are willing to comprehend at the moment."

She pursed her lips at him, a gesture he very much appreciated. Made him want to kiss those red cherry-puckers again—this time for hours. No more quickies for him! Next time he got his hands on Jessie—

"It's better than Duke's idea," Helen told Jessie. "He just wants us to grow the town organically. Like every person here of childbearing age could either adopt or become pregnant with the amount of children we'd need to grow this town. I'm so sick of the word organic I could scream."

"What would you do differently?" Jessie asked, and Zach was amazed that she was so interested.

"We suggested matchmaking balls and dances

and all kinds of things, but Duke was being selfish and didn't want other men around Liberty," Pansy said.

Liberty laughed. "I brought my business here, and that definitely brings customers to the saloon. Then we try to keep people by showing them the beautiful countryside and down-home warmth we offer."

Jessie looked at Zach. "Twins will definitely help, but it's no population explosion."

Was she suggesting more children? "No, it's not," Zach said, his mind working rapidly. "I'm willing to work on a population explosion with you."

The ladies giggled, but Jessie sent a frown his way. "You have all been very kind to me," she said, and the ladies smiled. "I'm sure you appreciate why I will probably not live here full-time with my children—"

"What?" Zach exclaimed, and the ladies began a nervous rustling. That pronouncement had to be worse than anything Duke had ever heard from Liberty! Maybe Holt was right. Although legalities were certainly something to be avoided... He'd much rather romance Jessie into seeing matters his way.

Jessie ignored his excitement. "Maybe my

family's company could have the next convention here."

The ladies looked at her, their faces wreathed in hopeful delight.

"No," Zach said. "I don't like makeup and cosmetics and face creams. Natural is the only way to go. But thank you for trying to help." He sat down heavily. "Our problem isn't women, we have plenty of those. There are few eligible bachelors, so the women have to look outside the town. Eventually, they move." He looked at Jessie. "Bet you thought I'd say yes just to keep you here."

She raised her chin. "I do not plan the conventions. I oversee them and give lectures."

"You're being hasty, Zach," Helen said. "Remember, we're all about commerce here, and commerce is commerce, even if it comes out of a bottle."

Zach blinked. It would never work. "This town is about women," he said slowly. "We need to showcase our women."

Pansy and Helen smiled, and the other ladies looked at him with appreciation.

"We have more to offer here than anywhere." He looked at Jessie. "You could do it. You could fix them up and make them beautiful, and we could be the most beautiful town in Texas, women-wise."

"They are beautiful," Jessie said. "Every woman here is unique and I've enjoyed meeting them."

"But most men, unlike myself, like the package. They like the bows on the package, too, the red lips and the fancy hair."

Jessie shook her head. "Zach, you don't understand."

"Tell me."

She got up. "I'm awfully tired all of a sudden, ladies. Thank you so much for your lovely gifts."

Somehow, he'd lost her attention. "I'll help you carry them to Helen's. The sidewalk is probably getting more slick, and I don't want you to fall. Now for the rest of you," he said, "is Duke coming back, or can I play taxi for you ladies?"

"You just take care of Jessie," Pansy said. "I'll call Duke to finish his driving duties. That means I get to watch the baby." Grinning, she went to the phone.

"Good night," Jessie said, hugging everyone in the room as she left. "Thank you so much for everything." Beside her, Zach carried out the gifts that had so warmed her heart. He'd completely surprised her by showing up, and then by basically offering himself in front of the ladies.

She'd learned a lot about him that she hadn't known, too.

But they were too different, they had different goals, and he'd lied to her. That reminded her very much of her ex, and she'd made a vow to herself that, if a man lied to her once, there were no second chances. She couldn't afford to make that mistake again.

She'd trusted Zach, and learned that he, too, told convenient fibs. She couldn't cut him any slack just because he'd lied to keep her in Tulips. "I've proven that I'd stay here willingly if I could," she said as they went through Helen's front door.

"Sensible of you," he said. "We're good people here."

She set her things down and took off her coat. "The jury is still out on you."

"Are you mad?"

She gave him a quizzical look. "What would you be, if our circumstances were reversed?"

"Hey, you hit my prize longhorn, and I didn't hold a grudge."

"Because the longhorn was still standing," Jessie said. "And we had sex."

He frowned. "We didn't have sex. We created children."

"I don't think you can be particularly sentimental about sex in the backseat of a car."

His frown grew deeper. "I damn sure can. I am very sentimental about that car! I've had it in storage for more than twelve weeks, a monument to the best sex I ever had!"

She blinked. "Really?"

"Well, hell yeah," Zach said. "Why? Didn't you think so?"

She tied her long hair up into a ponytail and pulled off her shoes. "I never did that in a car before, so I have no frame of reference."

"But you'd do it again? Wouldn't you?"

She glanced up at him. "With you?"

"You're sure as hell not ever making love to anyone else, Jessica T. Farnsworth," he said, "so don't waste your time considering your options."

She straightened. "That did not sound like a marriage proposal. It sounded like an order."

He nodded. "You didn't accept the proposal, so I have to declare limitations some other way."

"It's not going to work." Jessie moved into the kitchen, looking for Helen's teapot. "Marriage would make both of us crazy."

"We'd get to know each other better," Zach said, "and that's my whole goal."

"That's it?" She took down two teacups from the cabinet. "Shouldn't Miss Helen be here by now? You should check on her. It's very dangerous to be walking on the wet cement."

"See," he said, "you're starting to care about us. You're starting to take on Tulips' ways."

She shrugged. "I do care about Miss Helen and Miss Pansy. And some of the other ladies I've met."

He cleared his throat.

"Liberty, for example," she said. "And I'm pretty sure I'd like Pepper if I got to know her better."

He helped her put out cookies. "So, about this get to know us better thing," he said. "It probably works just as well for me as my sister."

"Maybe," she said, "but your sister isn't trying to tie me down."

Stubborn. But she had a point. "What if I didn't try to tie you down? What if I merely tied myself to you?"

She looked at him suspiciously. "I know you didn't mean that the way it sounded."

"I don't have Duke's handcuffs, if that's what you're worried about." He sat in the chair she pointed to. "How about if I move into wherever it is that you live?"

She shook her head at him. "Your ranch is here.

You would not enjoy my lifestyle. It's all travel, and you're a homebody."

He sensed an angle and perhaps an advantage. "So you can't take twins on the road with you."

"I can."

"Well, at first, maybe. But later on, they'll need stability. They can't get any better stability than here in Tulips." He took a slow sip of the hot tea, thinking how much he liked sitting here with Jessie, just the two of them talking about their future and their goals.

He'd get her to see his way eventually.

She looked at him. He sensed a struggle.

"Kids need schools and balance and ties to heritage," he said softly. He gazed at her, his fingers reaching out to cover hers on the table. "The girl who has everything ought to know that."

Chapter Nine

Jessie shook her head. "It's not quite like that. I've worked hard for everything I have. And I've always felt quite 'normal.'"

"I'm not sure that's the right word for you." Zach grinned. "Maybe 'exceptional.' There's the word I'm looking for."

"Well, it definitely seems exceptional to be having children with you," Jessie said, feeling uneasy. "This is probably not going to be the most graceful relationship between two people, considering how we've started out."

"I'm good with it," Zach said. "You'll be a great mother, I'll be an awesome dad. The babies will have interesting and varied lives." He gave her a slow, sexy grin. "You've definitely made my life interesting."

She nodded. "Still seeing the twins?"

He grinned again. "You're the only woman in my life now."

Her brow lifted. "How do I know you're not telling me a fib?"

"You can trust me. But because you think you can't, I'll tell you a secret no one in this town knows."

"Part of me is curious, and part of me says knowing anything more about you could be detrimental." *Mostly to my heart.*

"That suspicious streak of yours is going to interfere with our closeness," Zach said. "I'm sure you wouldn't want that to happen, for the sake of the children."

He was going to use that angle every chance he got. "Go on," she said, "tell the monumental secret."

"I have to trust you," he said.

"You're stretching our boundaries," she said. "All we've learned to do so far is distrust."

"Okay," he said with a mock frown, "but I don't share secrets with just anyone."

"I won't dignify that with a show of curiosity."

"The twins live in Dallas. They're writers."

Jessie blinked. "Interesting, if you like to read in bed, I guess."

"So suspicious," he said, laughing. "You're almost no fun to share a secret with."

"I never said I was fun," Jessie said. "I'm just learning to embrace stability."

"I write western romance," he said proudly. "They're my critique group."

She stared at him. "That's your secret?"

He nodded proudly. "Yep."

"It's a good one." Zach with a creative, cerebral side? It was almost hard to imagine. "You know, the Gang would love to know—"

"Hey!" He sat up. "You promised not to say anything."

"But it's so juicy and scandalous," she teased. "They'd love to know your mysterious side."

"We're bonding over secrets," Zach said. "The Gang is not to know."

"But they'd figure out a way to use your hobby to grow Tulips." She grinned at him. "Imagine your face on a billboard at the entrance of the city 'Tulips—Home Of Zach Forrester, Western Romance Writer.' You could turn this town into a haven for aspiring artists."

"It's not organic," Zach said.

"Maybe Duke doesn't get everything he wants.

And I might remind you, we are doing our part in the organic growth department, twice over."

"I should have known you'd go for the dramatic tie-down of my bachelorhood."

She shrugged. "So back to the billboard—"

"I notice you care about our town." Zach smiled. "You seem to be thinking deeply on our dilemma. This gives me hope for our future."

"Don't," Jessie said. "I could never marry a moody writer."

"That's a cliché." Zach bit into a cookie. "Just as much a cliché as women having moody times of the month."

Jessie opened her mouth to say she probably did, then closed it. She wouldn't be having one of those for a while, so there was no point in scaring him.

"You were going to say you had no moody times," Zach said. "I'm glad for that. Only one of us can be moody."

"What good does it do to write if no one knows you do it?" Jessie asked.

"I need that outlet for my soul. I can't not create. I started out with cowboy poetry, and one day, I realized my poem went on and on. It had taken on epic proportions but wasn't as good as

The Odyssey, for example. I feared, in fact, that it was pretty much lengthy dreck. I took it to a workshop and I met the twins, and they suggested a romance, and we've been together ever since."

Jessie tried not to be jealous of other women having a piece of Zach she would never share. "Should I read some of your work?"

He looked surprised. "Would you want to?"

"It would be a sampling, wouldn't it? Of your style?"

"You're trying to cheat," Zach said with a grin. "It won't work. You're going to have to learn about me through one-on-one communication."

They looked at each other for a long moment.

"Besides, I don't think western romance is your cup of tea," Zach told her. "I'll tell the babies bedtime tales of cowboys and Christmas carols, though."

"I never heard those."

He nodded. "I know. I sensed that the girl who had everything might not have experienced some of the best parts of life."

She leaned back in her chair. "I've always believed that people who make lasting bonds with each other are best suited if they have similar backgrounds."

"We're not exactly dissimilar. We're both the rogue elements in our families."

"I wish I could refute that," she said slowly. "Unfortunately, I only lately came into the family's good graces."

Zach grinned. "The old ladies can pick a winner every time."

"What does that mean?"

"It means," he said, "that they seem to know how to find diamonds in the rough."

"They did not find me," Jessie said, "I drove through this town. I don't want to believe that my future is based on my bad sense of direction."

He grinned. "I'm really looking forward to this."

"It's not going to work, Zach," Jessie said honestly. "My bad sense of direction applies to maps *and* men. They say once bitten, twice shy, and you've already proved yourself to be less than trustworthy. No bonding between us, no cajoling and teasing, can change the way I feel." She looked at him, wanting him to understand. "Everything I know tells me you're not a good bet for my life. While I realize nothing is a safe bet, now that I'm going to be a mother, I'm going to be making the best choices I possibly can."

ZACH LEFT Helen's house, knowing that he and Jessie were further apart than ever. It wasn't easy on a man who was afraid of being an absentee father.

He went home to the Triple F, wondering how he would ever convince Jessie that he was a good man, a man she wanted and needed in her life. All the lights were on at the house, which surprised him since it was quite late.

Pepper tugged an overstuffed suitcase out the front door as he walked onto the porch.

"Going somewhere?" he asked. "I can't advise it. The roads outside the ranch are slick."

Pepper shook her head. "I know. I'll be all right."

"I could drive you," he offered.

"No, thanks." She slid the heavy suitcase down the steps and then almost slipped.

"Pepper, this isn't your best idea. The most educated Forrester should know that."

Sighing, she stood upright, facing him as he stood at the top of the porch. "All right. You have a point."

"A damn good one," he said gruffly, going down the steps to retrieve the bag. "This is heavy! What the hell, Pepper?"

Once he reached the top of the stairs and set the case inside the door, she tugged it down the hallway. He followed her, bemused. "I suppose it's possible you're heading for a warmer place."

"Zach, could you mind your own business?" she snapped.

"Not usually," he said mildly. "It's a flaw in my personality, particularly where my sister is concerned."

She burst into tears. Zach blinked. "Damn, Pepper, is something wrong?"

"No. I just need to get out of here."

She was acting a lot like Jessie. "What the hell's the matter with all the females around here, anyway?"

"We all have lives that you men can't exactly comprehend," Pepper said, "because we're not being good little apron-wearing, dinner-fixing feetwarmers."

"Whoa," Zach said. "I only know five words in the female language. 'Let me get the kettle.'"

"That would be nice," Pepper said, sniffling as she finished dragging her suitcase off like a protective animal.

"It's the weather," Zach mused. "It's making everyone stir-crazy." Setting the kettle on to boil, he set out two teacups the way Helen and Pansy would. He felt proud of himself, and got a little more fancy by putting some chocolate chip cookies on the saucers. Whatever was ailing Pepper would surely go away when his sister saw his handiwork.

She came into the kitchen and sat at the table, grateful to let him handle tea-duty.

"It's the Christmas season," Zach pointed out. "We should be feeling tidings of joy. Not panic and stress."

Pepper shook her head. "I can't talk about it, so don't ask."

He poured the hot water into the teacups, setting one in front of her before he sat down. "I can talk about my dilemma, if you're in the mood to humor me."

"Shoot," Pepper said. "One of us might as well abuse the sibling privilege."

"Right." Zach burned his tongue, not paying attention to the heat in his cup as he sipped. "Last chance to spill before I grab the spotlight."

Pepper shook her head. There was no way she could talk about her secret. It wasn't time. Eventually, perhaps she could. But not now. Zach would be shocked. Duke would be stunned. Despite their own out-of-wedlock pregnancies, they would be beside themselves to learn of her own children.

She couldn't second-guess her decisions now.

The die had been cast long ago. "I am positive that if we spend this cold, rainy evening getting your issues addressed," Pepper said, "I'll feel better empathetically."

Zach hoped so. A less-selfish brother would insist that she let big bro shoulder her burden, but Pepper wasn't the type of girl who could be pushed.

"My problem is Jessie," he said. "She's having my children."

"I know," Pepper said. "I took a gift by. I look forward to having her in the family."

He frowned, completely startled.

"Well, I do," Pepper said. "She'll be a wonderful sister, just like Liberty."

"Do you know something I don't?" Zach asked. "Because when I left her forty-five minutes ago, she didn't want to have anything to do with me."

"Not you, maybe, but she's fine with me. And I'm the auntie. I'll occupy a glorious place in those little babies' lives." She smiled, pleased by the notion. "It's a wonderful Christmas present. I'll have two little Forresters to spoil and coddle, and when they turn into brats, you won't be able to blame Aunt Pepper because they'll love me too much."

Zach frowned. "They need to be Forresters."

"They'll be Farnsworth-Forresters," Pepper said. "Doesn't that sound pretty?"

"It's a mouthful," he said unhappily. "Pepper, I don't want to be a father who isn't married to the mother of my children. I want us to live under one roof. Does that make sense?"

Her brother touched a nerve inside her. But she doubted her teenage love would have shared Zach's sentiments. No one wanted to be tied down by children at that young age. "It makes sense," she said carefully. "I'm not really a good person to talk to about this."

"You're the best."

"No," Pepper said, getting up from the table with her teacup. "Believe me, you should talk to Helen and Pansy or Holt. I am no expert on anything except medical matters."

Since she'd just been on her way out the door to catch a redeye to visit her own twins, Toby and Josh, her advice was probably the worst Zach could receive. Far better for him to talk to someone with a success rate, like Duke.

She had to concentrate on her children and Christmas and the medical clinic she was start-ing, and how she was finally going to bring the boys home to Tulips without everyone she knew being completely ashamed of what she'd done so many years ago.

IN THE MORNING, Zach got up bright and early and went outside to the barn to check on Jessie's car. Molly-Jimbo slept in the back seat, so he shooed her out, not certain how she'd sneaked into the garage and gotten in. "You are the wiliest dog I ever met," he told the golden retriever. "Why can't you act like you're Duke's dog?"

Molly barked at a chicken and ran off, not bothered at all by Zach's lack of praise for her cunning.

He inspected the car, certain Jessie never had a long-haired dog sleeping in her precious land yacht. The best thing to do would be to take it into town, have it vacuumed and polished, hang a wreath on the grill and take it to her with an apology and a goodbye.

"But I'm a stronger man than that," he said, starting back toward the house. "I'm not going to let her scare me off with a wee little 'no.'"

After talking to Pepper last night, he'd realized he couldn't give up so easily. Not this time. Duke had hung in there until he won Liberty's heart—surely Forrester grit counted for something.

He had babies counting on his grit.

He felt good about deciding that determination would be his guide. The doorbell rang and his heart leaped—maybe Jessie had come to get her car at last. Or even better, perhaps she'd come to say that their future together, in whatever form or fashion, would be a bright one.

He hoped so. He was becoming quite fond of that sassy girl from the city.

Opening the door, he looked at the two tall, big-shouldered strangers on his porch. A faint sense of alarm trickled through him. Strangers didn't pass by this way often.

"Howdy," he said. "Can I help you boys?"

"We're looking for Zach Forrester," one of them said.

"I'm Zach," he said, and the men nodded their heads.

"Good," the other said, punching him square on the jaw.

Chapter Ten

Jessie heard a crack and a thump and realized her brothers had not been candid with their reasons for wanting to meet Zach. "You hurt him!"

She rushed forward and knelt beside Zach. "Are you all right?"

"I was better about five minutes ago," Zach said, rising to his feet. He looked at her brothers with a frown. "Settle your issues, boys, and move along."

"The issue is Jessie," one said, but Jessie put out a hand.

"No, I am not the issue. Apologize! Both of you. And introduce yourselves properly. Or I'm not leaving with you."

They shifted, glaring at Zach. "I'm serious," she said. "If you're going to be medieval about this, you might as well go home."

They took that comment in with frowns. Just when she thought this might be the first time her brothers didn't listen to her, they each put out a reluctant hand.

"Robert Farnsworth," the taller of the two said. "This is my brother Cedric."

Zach nodded. Jessie noticed he didn't touch his chin, which had to ache, judging by the redness on it and how hard Robert had hit him. "I am so ashamed of you," she told her brothers. "Zach, I do apologize. They've never acted like cavemen before."

"I'd invite you in," Zach said, "but you'd probably prefer to say your piece on the porch."

"Actually, we've said all we have to say," Robert said.

"Excellent." Zach nodded, handing Jessie's keys to her. "You know where your car is, Jessie. Glad you have someone to accompany you home. I won't worry about you."

He closed the door.

Jessie's jaw dropped. "Zach!" She wouldn't reduce herself to banging on a man's door to get his attention, but her heart jumped wildly inside her. "You did not help the situation," she told her brothers.

"I wasn't thinking," Robert said. "I'm sorry, Jessie. I've just been wanting to do that so badly ever since you told me what he did to you."

"He did exactly what I wanted him to," Jessie said between clenched teeth. "Oh, Pepper! I'm so glad you're here."

Pepper glanced up in the process of hauling a big bag out the door with her. "Hi, Jessie." She locked the front door and stood. "I'm Pepper Forrester," she said to Jessie's brothers. "You must be the reason I had to put a cold cloth on Zach's face."

"We should apologize," Robert said.

"Well, I don't think it'll matter." Pepper lugged the case down the steps. "He's not in a listening mood. Kind of funny and temperamental that way."

"Can I carry that for you?" Cedric asked.

"Oh, no," Pepper said. "We Forresters stick tightly together, so I'll have to forego the niceties you're offering. Goodbye, Jessie."

"Pepper!" Jessie exclaimed.

"This is kind of an odd bunch," Cedric said, watching Pepper wrestle with her huge bag on the way to her truck. "I feel like I'm on a set of *Gunsmoke*. Jessie, I don't know what you saw in that cowpoke."

Jessie whirled on her brothers. "Let's just get my car and go. You've quite destroyed any credibility with me and worn out your welcome in Tulips."

Robert walked down the porch. "I saw a saloon in town where we could get a bite to eat before we go back—"

"Don't even bother," Jessie said tightly. "You'd probably be served arsenic."

"Surely they don't get their feelings hurt that easily," Cedric said. "It was just a tap on the chin. A big strong cowboy can take a tiny knock."

Robert shrugged. "How do you expect us to feel? If it wasn't for him and his lack of polite gentleman's equipment—"

"Condoms," Cedric said.

"You'd be back with your—"

"No, I wouldn't," Jessie said. "Whatever came before Zach doesn't matter to me anymore."

"Jessie," Robert said, "this can't possibly work. You don't even know him. You come from different places. I can't see you living here."

Jessie shook her head. "Zach is a good man."

"He lied about your car. He took advantage of you. There's no good in that," Cedric pointed out.

"You're a lawyer," Jessie said. "Lies are something you've been known to—"

"Jessie," Cedric said, "we don't like him."

"That's tough," Jessie said. "I want you both to get back in the car you came to town in, and go home. I'm staying to fix this with the father of my children."

"Mom and Dad will be upset," Robert reminded her.

"I'll deal with that later," Jessie said. "Goodbye."

Robert and Cedric stepped off the porch. "Call us if you change your mind. We'll be here—"

"I have a car. I'm not a prisoner." Jessie raised her chin, a sisterly thought coming to her. "On second thought, be certain you stop in at the Tulips Saloon on the way out. You just can't beat their coconut cake."

Cedric perked up. "I love coconut cake."

"This one is so heavenly and light that you barely taste the coconut. It's more like fluffy sweetness you can't describe."

Robert nodded. "I'm hungry."

"Good. You'll like it."

"What if he doesn't let you in?" Cedric asked.

"Oh, Zach will let me in." Jessie looked upstairs. "Don't worry about me."

Grumbling about leaving her behind, her overprotective brothers got in their Lincoln Town Car and drove away. As soon as they were out of sight, she turned to knock on the door. It was snatched from her fingertips before she could, and Zach's strong hand pulled her inside.

He locked the door and kissed her passionately, his mouth all over hers, hard and searching. Then he pushed her away.

"Just in case you think I'm being a coward by not fighting back," he said, "I don't fight with relatives, even future relatives who behave badly."

"They weren't truthful to me. They said they just wanted to meet you," Jessie said.

"Now they have. I'll always remember my first Christmas holiday with your family."

"Hold that thought." She pulled her cell phone from her purse. "What is the number to the Tulips Saloon?"

He told her and she dialed quickly. "Pansy," she said, looking at Zach, "I was hoping you'd be there. No, I don't need anything, but I was going to let you know that two very handsome, very eligible bachelors are on their way to try your coconut cake."

She smiled as Pansy told Helen to make sure she had two large slices for the men. "I knew you'd take care of it. Thank you, Pansy."

Clicking off the phone, she smiled at Zach. "They're calling several of Tulips' most eligible ladies to visit the newcomers."

"Excellent revenge," Zach said. "Your brothers are about to get everything they deserve. I didn't know lawyers were such physical types. Maybe a lawsuit, a custody skirmish—"

"No," Jessie said, "there'll be none of those."

"Good," Zach said. "Holt suggested it, but it's been years since anyone in this town has practiced law."

"Was anyone in Tulips ever involved in the legal profession?"

"Duke has mostly been the town scales of justice," he said. "I believe I was in the middle of kissing you—"

Jessie put a hand on his chest to stop him. "No."

"Kissing is still sex for you?"

She gave him a wry look. "I think we're past that point. Kissing is the least of my worries. My brothers brought up an important point."

"This should be good." Zach crossed his arms.

"I'm very, very reserved around men I don't know, and I may have been under the opposites attract theory when I, when we—"

"I like where this is heading," Zach said. "I've

never been a woman's fantasy before. At least I don't think."

She rolled her eyes. "We need to shed the illusions."

"God, I hope so." Zach gave her dress a tiny tug. "I want you to shed a lot around me."

"I'm moving in," Jessie said.

"Tulips will be scandalized," Zach said with a grin.

"WHAT WE NEED," Pansy said, the next day when it seemed things were more quiet around Tulips, "is to help Pepper meet a man. This is where we're going wrong."

Helen and Pansy sat inside the Tulips Saloon, sharing a companionable cup of tea now that all the day's customers had left and the store was closed. This was home away from home, their very favorite place to relax and enjoy friendships.

"I thought perhaps Jessie's brothers might have been prime candidates," Helen said thoughtfully, "but the Tulips' ladies so fawned on them that their dance cards would be totally full should they ever return."

Pansy giggled. "They won't. They know what's

waiting for them if they do. Our girls would get them to the altar."

Helen nodded. "The problem with Pepper is that the only man she ever fell for was—"

"Highly inappropriate." Pansy stared down into her teacup. "I had so many hopes for Luke McGarrett when he was a child. He turned into such a rascal."

"Poor Pepper. So intelligent, such a model of responsibility, and the man who breaks her heart is—"

Helen shook her head. "Good thing he never returned to Tulips. I hear he made a fortune doing something nefarious. It's always the good that attracts the bad."

Pansy adjusted her spectacles. "I don't know where we'd find the man who deserves Pepper, anyway. So let's work on Jessie."

Two sharp raps on the window caught their attention. Hiram and Bug stood outside, waving urgently.

"They want tea," Pansy said.

"Of course they do." Helen got up to let them in. "It's cold outside, and we made cookies, besides."

She unlocked the door and the men darted in.

"What is it?" Helen asked.

"We've got news," Hiram said.

"Whatever it is, we've probably already heard it," Pansy said. "I do hope we haven't."

"We're going to throw an impromptu Christmas parade," Bug said. "I couldn't get over the idea of a parade. Me and Mrs. Carmine will ride at the front on our bays, and Hiram's gonna dress up as the fat white, whiskered man in the red cap and throw candy."

They all considered Hiram, who was thin as a rail and had no decent throwing arm as far as any of them knew.

"Okay," Helen said. "Did Duke approve this quilted plan of yours?"

"We're not going to ask him." Bug looked over his shoulder through the window toward Duke's office. "He'll just say no. We're going to have the parade, and when he asks why we didn't tell him, we're going to say we left him a permit request but perhaps he was too busy with the baby and his brother's T-bird-stealing ways to notice it."

"Forgiveness instead of permission," Pansy said. "I should have a problem with that, but I don't."

"And what's our goal?" Helen asked.

"To put Tulips on the map. To bring the outside to us. Heck, Duke's keeping us all in the Dark Ages,"

Hiram complained. "We need the light of progress to come to this town, at least before I expire."

"You are getting rather long in the tooth," Helen agreed, for the hundredth time. "Pansy, you could be Mrs. Claus, and we could ask Jessie to judge the floats. If she's still here."

"Floats?" Bug wrinkled his face. "What floats?"

"What was the parade going to be, Bug?" Helen looked at him. "You and Mrs. Carmine riding horses, and Hiram bringing up the rear with a tiny sack of peppermints to throw at…my stars, we don't have any children here. What would be the point?"

Pansy sighed. "As usual, there is no point. It'll have to wait until Duke's child is old enough to catch a piece of candy."

"A parade with no children would be sacriledge," Hiram agreed. "I hadn't considered that. I thought people might bring their youngsters and see what a nice town we have."

"But if no one came, then—" Pansy began, and they all fell silent.

"Is Jessie still here?" Hiram asked.

"Last I heard, she was visiting Zach. Apparently, her brothers went to help her pick up her car and gave Zach a little tap on the chin."

"So is the car still here?" Hiram asked. "We could take our parade into Dallas, if we borrowed her car."

They all stared at him.

"It'd be even better if she'd drive us. She could be our town princess," Hiram said. "Every town has a princess of something. Like a harvest princess, or a snow princess."

Helen blinked. "It's advertising."

"She looks all citified," Bug pointed out. "She's pretty, and her car is awesome."

"I don't think we should use someone for their car," Pansy said.

"We could use Duke's squad car," Hiram said, and they all groaned.

"Why don't you hold that thought, Hiram?" Pansy said, and they all smiled so he wouldn't have his feelings hurt. "Our first Christmas parade should be less formal-looking, and a pink car is very festive."

"It's just the right color for Tulips!" Helen exclaimed. "Why didn't I think of that before?"

"Because we never thought about taking our parade to the city," Pansy said, "and then we wouldn't need Duke's permission."

"We could decorate it all fancy, and put a sign on the side that reads 'Come To The Tulips Saloon For Christmas Memories And A Chance At A

Thousand-Dollar Santa Sack,'" Pansy said, which earned her three shocked expressions.

"Where would we get that kind of money?" Bug asked.

"Perhaps we'd offer donations in the sack. Like, maybe a wedding gown or services from Liberty's Lace, and maybe cookies from our saloon, and we have many talented ladies who can do all sorts of things here," Pansy said reasonably. "If all fifty of us chipped in four bucks, that'd be two hundred dollars right there."

They considered that for a few moments.

"I have four bucks," Hiram said.

"Who would be the one to ask Jessie?" Bug asked.

"We would," Helen said. "You keep Zach busy. He might tell Duke, or he might get weird on us about Jessie removing her car from his barn. So far, and through twists of fate, he's managed to keep her prized possession in his barn, which I suspect makes him very happy."

"So Jessie's would be the lead car, and there'll be no horses, which will make Mrs. Carmine sad, but she'll understand," Bug said thoughtfully.

"We can take Molly-Jimbo. We'll put a Santa cap on her head, and the kids will love that," Pansy suggested.

"And we'll pack the willing ladies from our town into trucks that follow Jessie's car," Helen said.

"It's crazy," Hiram said. "Wouldn't we have to have a Dallas permit?"

"For three or four cars?" Helen asked. "We'd be out of there so quickly, no one would think it was a parade. We're just leaving calling cards that advertise our town as a great place to live. Which it is."

"But men don't come out for wedding dresses, which is what you're giving away," Hiram said reasonably. "They'd beat a hasty path out here for land, though."

"Duke would not be happy about that," Pansy said. "It's not organic growth."

"Bachelor land-grabs." Helen thought over that a moment. "Someone call Zach and ask a member of the young set if they'd go for that."

Pansy picked up the phone and dialed. "Oh. Hello, Jessie," she said. "Didn't I dial the Forresters? Oh, I did. So, you're still in town. Ah. Oh, how nice. All right. Thank you. Goodbye, dear."

She hung up, looking at Helen. "We'll have to put the parade off for a year or so due to lack of car and Tulip Princess, I believe. Zach and Jessie are leaving town. They're eloping."

Chapter Eleven

"I wouldn't be doing this if my brothers hadn't been so heavy-handed," Jessie said. Zach drove her car and she sat beside him, enjoying the midnight ride out of Tulips. Because it was two weeks until Christmas, and the weather was still cold and rainy, they had the top up on the convertible. But she didn't care. She could see the stars in the sky and she was on a new adventure in her life.

Change always made her happy.

"They were heavy-handed, indeed," Zach said. "Right on my jaw. So I'm completely for whatever suits your bad-sister adventurous side."

"Thanks," Jessie said. "I think." She gave him a considering look. "Do you think you'll encourage our children to be wayward as well?"

"One of us will. It'll be a toss-up as to which of us will be the more steadying influence."

"Hmm." She sighed. "I don't see a future for us."

"Of course you don't. You left your crystal ball with your magic mirror."

"Were you trying to make a joke?" Jessie asked. "A pointed reference to my line of work?"

"Nah. I'm just saying we're probably not meant to be together, so we shouldn't worry about that part. Legalizing us for the sake of the children is a good thing, though, and it'll mean we won't totally scandalize the little old tyrants of Tulips."

Jessie laughed. "They're not tyrants, and you love them."

"Yes. But even you recognize that living together under one roof without legal commitment would send them into plotting overdrive."

"Yes," Jessie said. "Our elopement should make everyone relax."

"Except you and me." Zach patted her leg, then tried to reach a sneaky hand under her skirt, which she expertly batted away. "I don't think I'll ever relax around you."

"Really?"

"You make me very crazy in an uncomfortable

way. I see you, and I want to kiss you. I smell you, and I want to hold you. I touch you, and I want to undress you. How's that for crazy?"

"Pretty much all in," Jessie said, secretly touched.

"So, you can tell me you feel the same way about me," Zach said, obviously hinting for attention.

She smiled. "I could, but I wouldn't be honest."

"Oh, man. I knew you were the kind of girl who wouldn't want to stroke my ego."

Jessie laughed. "You're right. I don't." Although she did have all the feelings he'd admitted to. She just wasn't ready to share those emotions. Her heart was still too raw; her pride wanted conviction that Zach wanted her, really wanted her.

For her children, she wanted to know that this man wouldn't change his mind on her, the way her ex had, and it seemed smart to make certain she was making a responsible choice.

"You're going to like being married to me, Jesssie."

"I am?" She raised a brow.

"Yes." He nodded. "We just need to make a covenant between us."

"Like what?"

"We agreed on a marriage compromise. I wanted the children to have my name, and be able to grow up in Tulips without everyone knowing they were the kids whose parents couldn't get their act together. And you wanted a trial period since we don't know each other."

"This is all very sensible," Jessie said, feeling very good about being orderly about her life for once. "Except I don't remember us covering the part about the children living in Tulips. My parents would be crushed, I think."

Zach was quiet for a moment. "I hadn't considered the parent factor. I need to meet your parents before we get married, even if it is only temporary."

Jessie hesitated. Zach in her world would likely not be a good thing. He'd already met her brothers, if that painful meeting could be called an introduction.

"Don't tell me. Your parents feel the same way your brothers do."

"I will admit that they're not exactly thrilled. They don't know you, and…"

"And I'm not from their social circle." He took his hand from her leg and put it on the steering wheel. "Maybe we're heading in the wrong direction."

"No. We're on the road to Las Vegas and the Elvis impersonator you said you wanted to marry us."

Zach shook his head. "We need to head to your folks, Jessie. It would be bad manners on my part not to ask your father for your hand in marriage."

Stunned, Jessie blinked away tears that rose unexpectedly. It was very sweet of Zach, very gentlemanly, to say such a thing. The veneer of realness he was trying to put on their situation stole her breath, and more significantly, pieces of her heart.

It was too much, too soon, after her recent breakup.

"Zach, I'd rather elope," she said quietly.

"Tell me why."

"It's hard to put into words—"

"Not really. I'm a guy who likes plain words and reasoning. Be honest about what you're thinking."

Be honest. Her whole career was spent on making things pretty, showing anything unflattering in the best possible light. "My parents were crazy about—"

"Yes, yes. Okay. The guy you left at the altar was their kind."

"I didn't exactly leave him," Jessie said. "I had a choice. He was having an affair with a woman from a rival firm. I could have glossed it over and married him and hoped for the best. But covering up my feelings isn't as easy as covering up scars, stretch marks and blemishes." She looked at him. "My parents advised me to marry him, that the affair was wedding nerves."

"No," Zach said quietly. "It was a guy being a jerk, wanting to have his cake and eat it, too, and getting away with it pretty well."

"That's what I thought," Jessie said happily, pulling out a bag of pretzels for them to share and cracking open a Coke for him and a bottle of orange juice for her. "So it seemed much more sensible to me to live through the humiliation of calling off a wedding."

"I like your sensible side."

"Which is why you have to listen to me about my parents. They're not going to like you. They're just kind of that way."

"Why? Because I won't sleep with your rivals, girlfriends or anyone else while we're married?"

She blinked. "Would you want to?"

"Hell, no. Why would I, when I've got you?"

"Are you perfect?" Jessie asked. "I have to tell you, I keep looking for your flaws, and you're annoyingly short of them."

"No, I'm not," Zach said. "I told you, the men

in our town live by the reputation of our sins. Remember that conversation?"

"Yes," Jessie said, "but I'm starting to not believe you."

"Trust me, you'll find plenty about me that is imperfect."

"Good. I'm much more enthralled by imperfect these days. It's safer."

"What's your parents' address?"

Jessie sighed. "You're right. You're not perfect."

She could see him grinning widely by the lights of passing cars. "We'll be needing an airport."

"I like driving. We can get to anywhere."

"We can't get to Bermuda in this mode of transportation," Jessie pointed out.

"No, we can't," Zach said. "I'll be the first man in Tulips who had to go out of the country to meet a bride's parents."

"Are you okay with that?"

"Yes, except I'm not a good flier."

She laughed. "That's why my parents gave me this wonderful car. I drive just about everywhere I can. I like to see the countryside, and I like to meet people."

"Okay." Zach nodded. "So we could get married in Bermuda, I guess."

"No. That's the one thing you have to promise me. We do this temporarily, with no pomp and circumstance, just like we planned, after you meet my parents."

"I agree," Zach said, "only because I want the mother of my children to be happy."

"Thank you." Jessie pulled her phone from her purse. "Where's the nearest airport?"

"We're approximately one hour east of Dallas. So I would say DFW."

She dialed numbers on her phone. "Hi, Mom. Yes, everything's fine. I'd like to bring someone home to meet you. That sounds wonderful. Thank you. Yes, I love you, too. Tell Daddy I love him." She hung up and looked at Zach. "My brothers had business in Dallas that they attended to, so the company plane is still at the airport. They're going to hold it for us."

"So I'm going to be flying on the same private plane with your brothers?" Zach asked.

She smiled. "You asked to meet my parents."

"Yes, I did. And I'm looking forward to it."

"I have to warn you, they're a little frosty at first. Definitely not as warm as the people of Tulips. But they'll be on their best behavior."

Zach grinned and didn't say a word as he turned

the car around. Jessie looked out the window, thinking that surely, on the road to the altar, the second time was a charm.

"MOTHER, FATHER, this is Zach Forrester," Jessie said to her parents, who stood tall and elegant in the doorway of their Bermuda home.

Zach had survived the plane trip with Jessie's two brothers without incident. He didn't care what they thought about him. But that was the easy part. He did want Jessie's parents to like him. Deep inside, he knew she was the girl for him.

Her parents didn't look so convinced.

"Hello, Zach," Mrs. Farnsworth said. Mr. Farnsworth merely nodded.

They weren't snobby, Zach decided, merely unhappy and perhaps surprised by the turn of events. He could understand that, so he gave them a chance to warm up to him.

They never did. Dinner was a quiet affair. He was seated across from Jessie at the table, though that was fine because he could enjoy looking at her. She'd dressed a little fancy for dinner, in a red dress with cleavage and glittering diamond earrings. He had only one change of clothes with him, since they'd planned on going to Vegas.

Jeans had probably never been worn to dinner at this table.

The brothers ignored him, as they had on the plane.

He shrugged all that off. Whether they liked it or not, they were going to be family for the rest of their lives. Like a bucking bronc, he would let them have their head until they calmed down. If the shock ever wore off and they did ease up, he'd be the first to extend a hand of friendship.

"What do you do, Zach?" Mrs. Farnsworth asked.

"A lot of ranching, mostly. My ranch is in a small town in Texas called Tulips."

"Jessie, I can't imagine what you were doing there," her mother said. "Did you take a wrong turn?"

"I think…I took the right turn for me," Jessie said, and Zach gave her a smile.

Mrs. Farnsworth laid down her fork, all pretense at gentility evaporating. "I just don't understand how this happened. How could you have gotten our daughter pregnant? She doesn't even know you. We don't know you. For heaven's sakes, Jessie, this man could be a…a—"

"Mother," Jessie said. "I'm going to go lie down. It's been a long day."

They all stood. Zach looked at Jessie, worried.

"May will take you to your room, Zach," Mrs. Farnsworth said. "The driver will take you back to the airport in the morning at eight o'clock."

All of Jessie's family merely stared at him silently. Zach realized he'd been dismissed.

"The driver will be taking me and Jessie to the airport," he said, his voice measured and quiet. "We're getting married. I came here to ask you for your daughter's hand in marriage, sir. Whether or not you give it willingly, I suppose, is up to you." He nodded to them and followed May down the hall with a last look at Jessie.

She'd turned very pale, a startling contrast to her red gown.

He closed the door, looked around the well-appointed room and sighed before pulling his boots off and sitting down in a chair to think.

IN THE NIGHT, Zach heard his bedroom door open. Squinting at his watch, he saw it was two o'clock in the morning. He lay very still, waiting to see who his visitor was.

The person quietly closed the door, then crept to the king-size bed. Luckily for him, he'd chosen to sleep on the side farthest from the door. He held his breath.

Whoever it was had a sincere lack of courage. They, too, seemed to be holding their breath.

He felt his blanket turn back, then something soft and warm slipped into the bed next to him.

Jessie.

"Zach," she whispered.

He felt his heart speed up. If her parents caught her in here with him, there'd be bad feelings for years. Maybe he should just fake sleeping, for her sake, and then she'd go away.

She slid up against him, curling her head against his chest. "Zach," she whispered, "Bermuda is a wonderful place to spend Christmas."

Chapter Twelve

Zach rolled over on her, pinning her beneath him. Surprised, she shivered.

"Are you asking, making a comment or have you been set up to lure me to stay here?"

"All of the above," she whispered.

"No," he said, kissing her. "We're sticking to the original plan. I don't like your folks, and they don't like me, and you knew that's exactly what would happen. I've done the right thing by meeting your father and asking for your hand. I never said I cared whether he gave me his blessing or not. Now we move on to Vegas, and then home sweet home to Tulips."

He kissed her hard and then softly, enjoying her lips and making her want him. She ran her hands along his back, shocked to find him naked.

"You have one last chance to run out of here, little Red Riding Hood," he said. "If you stay, we're really going to shock your family. I promise."

A shudder of delight tingled her body. "You're crazy."

"Yes, I am. You knew that about me, so there's been no surprises from my side. You, on the other hand, didn't exactly tell me your situation."

"I told you we were from different worlds."

"And luckily, you fit my world just fine, because that's where we'll be spending our time."

Jessie pulled him close. "Let's not talk about plans for the future right now."

He nipped at her lower lip gently. "Your brothers could rush in here any minute, determined to shoot me for dishonoring their sister in their home, and you don't want me tying you down?"

Jessie giggled. "My brothers aren't that bad." He was kissing down her neck to her chest, making her crave him even more. "Are you going to make love to me?"

"I can't decide. It would probably pale next to doing it in the back of your car in the open air under the sun. It's so stuffy in this house, I feel like I'm in a cage."

"It's not stuffy. It's—"

"I don't do stuffy, and neither do you, Jessie, which explains why you live out of a carpetbag, drive a convertible and stay on the road most of the time."

She went still. "I never thought of it that way."

"Because they kept you busy with a promotion? An atta-girl for staying in the family fold?"

"No, I really am good at what I do."

"I believe that. I just don't think you need all the family props to be what you are."

She pushed him off her. "What are you saying?"

"I'm saying you don't have to let them send you in here to plead their case for them."

"True." She sat beside him, and he knew she was staring down at him. "We have a lot to talk about."

He pulled her down next to him and held her tight. "We're going to shock May in the morning when she finds you in here. That'll be my answer to your parents—nothing is separating us. Not them, not the meatheads playing rough, which they didn't do very well, I'll have to say. I got hit harder on the playground."

"I must have missed your stubborn, determined side."

"Then you missed my best side," he said, kissing

her neck. "One day, Jessica Tomball Farnsworth, you're going to be glad my bull stopped your car from its speeding path to nowhere."

She pinched him. "My life has not been no-where."

He grunted. "If you pinch me again, I'm going to take that as a call of the wild to make love to you."

"You could, you know."

"I could. But I'm not going to because we're not married yet, and I don't want you to want me just for sex. Now don't beg anymore, it's not ladylike."

She gave a backwards kick, hitting him squarely on his leg, but he just tugged her up against him closely so that she lay in the crook of his body. There was warmth, and hardness and affection wrapped all around her, it was giving and not taking, so Jessie closed her eyes.

This one is different.

In the morning, Zach and Jessie stood on the tarmac, preparing to board the Farnsworth jet.

"You need to be here for the holidays," her mother said.

"You need me to be here?" Jessie asked. "If last night was any indication of how happy the holidays would be around here, I'd be better off somewhere else." She hugged her mother. "Good-bye, Mom."

"We invited him," her father said as she hugged him.

"This isn't about you," Jessie said. "It's about me and Zach, and the life we're building together. So far, my brothers have punched him and you've treated him like he's committed a crime, when all he wanted was to come here and show you respect. I'm lucky he's still talking to me. Goodbye, Daddy."

"We'll come to the wedding," her mother said, but Jessie shook her head.

"It's better this way. We're having an Elvis impersonator officiate, and I don't think you'd be comfortable, Mother."

Her parents looked stricken. Jessie gave them a soothing smile. "It's going to be all right. It really is. This is going to turn out so much better than the future I had planned."

"But what kind of future do you have planned? Have you thought about anything beyond the children?" her father protested.

Jessie looked at Zach. "Not really. But that's the way we've planned our marriage, so we'd call that a success."

Zach helped her onto the jet. "Are you all right?"

"Yes," Jessie said, turning around to wave goodbye to her family. "I feel strangely grateful to you."

"Always a good thing," Zach said happily. "What do they serve on this flying turkey? I'm starved."

Jessie shook her head. "Just about anything you want. Ask."

"I could get used to traveling like this. Maybe I'll let my wife keep her job."

Jessie smiled. "Maybe I'll let my husband keep his."

Zach bit into an apple. "You make more money than me?"

Jessie laughed. "Money's not important in our relationship. We have enough issues to work out."

"Can this jet take us straight to Vegas?" Zach asked. "There's a woman I'm in a hurry to marry."

She blinked. "I never thought about it, but yes."

He tossed his apple core into a bag and leaned his head back, closing his eyes. "I feel like a kid on Christmas morning. I'll have a wife by sundown."

Jessie put her head back and closed her eyes, too, deciding napping was a good idea. She needed time to conceptualize actually becoming a bride. Not wanting to hurt Zach's feelings, she hadn't let on to how much her parents' disapproval bothered her. They were right: there was no future in their marriage. It was planned to be short and sweet.

Something inside her felt uneasy about that. A vague tickling of disappointment, and perhaps concern, made her stomach slightly nervous. "Oh. My father sent this along for you." She handed Zach a large brown envelope.

"What is it?"

"I have no idea."

He opened it, his face studious. "Papers signing away any rights to Farnsworth properties, businesses, monies, etc., etc."

Her heart stilled in her chest as Zach continued reading.

With a shrug, he pulled a pen from his jacket pocket and signed the documents. Shoving them back inside the envelope, he handed it to her and promptly went back to sleep.

Jessie's jaw went slack. He could have no idea he'd just signed a prenup that excluded him from millions of dollars. She stared at the envelope in her hands. A great part of her wanted to tear it to shreds; the other sensible part of her knew that her parents were being careful.

Zach didn't care about money at all. And while part of her admired his lack of fiscal greed, she knew he was merely sticking to their agreement to divorce after the birth of the twins.

He appeared to be completely prepared to keep his side of the bargain, which worried her more than made her happy—a surprising shift in her emotions, warning of a heart that might be broken a second time.

Jessie closed her eyes and tried not to think about Zach not feeling the same way about her as she was beginning to feel about him.

THE WEDDING was going to be short and sweet. They didn't have an Elvis impersonator because Zach had never really intended to do that. But he was aware Jessie might spook easily, so he'd fed her that story to make her try to see the marital mission in a light way.

This was a bride he intended to keep at the altar, and he'd learned the hard way by watching his brother's pain. Plus, he knew Jessie had a running streak in her, and after meeting her family, he sensed a reason for her to be headstrong.

"This is a good thing," he told her, gazing down at her as they stood in the chapel.

"I know." Jessie nodded.

"You can trust me," Zach said. "You're going to like living in Tulips."

Jessie shook her head. "I'm not living in Tulips."

The minister cleared his throat. "Are we ready?"

They stared at each other.

"We'll work it all out," Zach said. "Beyond the babies, everything else is just details."

"Major details." Jessie blinked back sudden tears, and Zach feared he might be losing her.

"Get a move on, sir," he said. "My bride suffers from cold feet. I intend to keep them warm for her."

The minister smiled. "We love a quick wedding in Vegas, but we also understand if you need a moment to collect yourself, young lady."

Jessie shook her head. "I'm all right. Thank you."

The minister cleared his throat, saying a lot of words Zach didn't hear, but what he did hear was Jessie's soft voice saying, "I do."

They were the sweetest two words he'd ever heard.

He kissed her to seal the deal.

But it was more than a deal, and his heart kicked hard in his chest to remind him of that. He was never going to get over falling for Jessie.

It was up to him to convince her.

———

THE MOMENTARY FEAR gripping Jessie as she stood beside Zach at the altar wouldn't go away. Even when the minister asked her if she needed a moment to collect herself, Jessie knew a moment wouldn't be enough to do the job. Considering what her family had put Zach through, she was surprised he still wanted her. This was not a man who was going to fall into another set of arms. He wasn't going to leave her. He'd said that in the beginning, and he was clearly a man of his word.

They flew back to Dallas in silence. Zach stared out one window of the jet, and she wondered about the man she'd married. Zach would never have wanted to marry her if she hadn't been pregnant, and that thought bothered her more than anything.

Her parents' worries worked in her mind.

Unconsciously, she touched her stomach, and the reasons why her life was changing much faster than it ever had before. "Beyond organic," she said, "another way to grow Tulips might be fish."

Zach turned to stare at her. "You have me hooked."

An unwilling smile tugged at her lips. "Impressed as I am by your clever repartee, I'm putting forth a genuine idea which may not be as good as building an elementary school, but one which draws men."

"Fish."

She nodded. "Fishing and needlepoint are two of life's most rewarding activities, as well as its greatest frustrations. Both require patience."

"We have little of that in Tulips, I'll warn you."

"In a town overpopulated by women? I doubt that."

He shook his head. "Please outline your plan for me."

"A Great Catch contest. Give away a fabulous prize for the biggest fish caught on the nearest lake. The twist is, every gentleman who enters has to take on board his boat one woman from Tulips to teach her to fish. She must be the one who catches the fish, down to putting the worm on the hook."

"That's almost cruel, and yet somehow genius," Zach said.

Jessie leaned her head back and closed her eyes. "That night, we have a fish fry on our land. Notice I said *our* land."

"I did, and I'm shocked." Zach shook his head. "The council of elders is going to give you a key to the city for that idea."

Jessie smiled to herself. All she needed was a key to Zach's heart. She'd leave the baiting and casting to the other ladies—she'd caught the man she wanted, at least for the next few months.

His approval warmed her and gave her hope for their coming family of four.

Chapter Thirteen

Four hours later, Zach took Jessie into his house, realizing they hadn't discussed sleeping arrangements. Setting down the suitcase she'd brought from the plane, he looked at his new bride. "Excuse me." Lifting her up, he went back out the door and carried her over the threshold.

"Nice," she said. "That was smooth, even for you."

"Just making sure I observe all the traditions. We're into traditions here."

She walked over to the Christmas tree. "I'll help you finish decorating this tomorrow. You never got past the candy canes."

"And no one else is going to do it, that's for sure." Zach shook his head. "I'll take the help, gladly. I suppose we should also discuss sleeping arrangements."

Jessie didn't look at him. "We can discuss it."

"I liked the one we had last night."

She turned to him. "The one where I sneak into your bed in the middle of the night?"

"That would work. Or you could start out there. It's up to you. We're married now, and I could even offer you the benefits of marriage."

She seemed embarrassed, and he liked it when she blushed.

"Do you realize we're a week from Christmas?" he asked softly. "And I've already gotten the best gift in the world." With one finger, he reached out to gently touch her hair.

"Sometimes your intensity is…unnerving."

A slow grin curved his mouth. "Ever since I met you, I've felt unnerved. This is not like me."

"I believe you." She hesitated. "When we agreed on a temporary marriage, it made sense to me to have the children born with your name. Not illegitimate."

He frowned. "It made more than sense. It was the only thing to do."

"I agree," she said quickly. "But if we share a marriage bed, it's going to feel a lot more real. Intimate. Not like we had an agreement."

"I see your point." He looked at her. "This thought must have occurred to you last night."

She nodded.

Holding her had been very intimate. He'd liked it. He'd held her as tight and close as he could—all night. "And you're not ready for that."

"It's hard when we barely know each other. And this time that we're married is our getting-to-know-each-other trial period."

"I do like sticking to agreements," Zach said. "A man is only as good as his word."

"It's more than an agreement. It's necessary. Everything about us is completely opposite."

"I hear your parents talking," he murmured.

"Maybe," she admitted. "They're a bit on the cool side, but they want me to be happy in the end."

"So do I." Zach nodded. "All right. Separate rooms it is, mother of my twins."

She stared at him. "Zach, I'm not going to say that my family was cordial with you. I'm embarrassed that they sent a prenup for you to sign." Uncertainty crossed her face, shadowing her eyes. "All the same, I'd like to thank you for understanding them."

They looked at each other for a long moment

before Zach shrugged. "I really couldn't care less about them or their money. I'm only interested in you."

She didn't say anything. There was nothing left to say. So he picked up her bag and carried it down the hall to a guest room. "You'll find everything you need in there. My room's upstairs, so…"

He'd been about to say "we basically have our own separate apartments," but the stricken look on her face stopped him. "So make yourself at home," he finished.

"Thank you," she said.

Nodding, he left her to settle in.

THEY WERE MOVING too fast. Zach recognized that. Or at least he was moving too fast to suit Jessie. If he were in her shoes, he'd probably feel the same, and since the goal was to keep her from freaking out, he'd decided to head upstairs to his bachelor bed.

They'd bought plain gold bands in Vegas. He thought that was the right decision, since she was determined to keep their marriage temporary. Diamonds would have said "I love you" and he didn't want to say anything she didn't want to hear.

There was nothing worse than someone forcing

emotions on a person that they didn't want to know about.

He'd have to wait to romance her. The two of them were alone in the house, so if he was patient, maybe he'd get a signal that she was beginning to feel secure in what they meant to each other.

Until then, he was going to be one hot and bothered cowboy.

THE NEXT DAY, Zach met Jessie at the breakfast table. Surprised, he saw that she'd set out two plates, each piled with eggs, bacon and steaming hot biscuits.

"Hungry?" she asked.

"Of course." Zach shook his head. "Did you do this because you like to cook or because you felt you had to?"

She turned to look at him, putting down the skillet she'd been drying. "Because I never get to cook."

"Oh," he said, sitting down to dig in. "Because I was hoping you were going to say 'I did it because I thought you'd like it,' and then I could say something manly like, 'Oh, you don't need to do that for me. I can cook for myself.'"

She raised a brow at him. "Can you?"

"Yes. Not as good as this, though." He began to shovel the food. "Much better than mine."

"I wouldn't have thought you were the kind of guy who could cook." She sat across from him.

"I can. Outdoors, indoors, it doesn't matter. I can gut a deer and get the venison ready for— Jessie, what's wrong?" He watched as she slipped from the room, putting down his fork in concern. The powder room door closed quickly, and he could hear Jessie being ill.

What to do now? If it were him, his mother would have offered him a cold cloth, or something, but he didn't know what to do except wait.

His stomach churned with worry.

A few moments later, she headed outside. He found her sitting on the porch. "Are you all right?"

"I am now. I shouldn't have cooked breakfast, I think. The bacon did it for me, and then, the story about the deer. I am a city girl, you know. I'm not going to be able to, you know."

"Oh, the g-word."

"Right. Some wives might be good with that, but I'm not going to be able to handle that stuff."

He reached to hold her hand, which was somewhat clammy. "I'm sorry. I've never known a pregnant woman before, except Liberty, and none of us knew much about her pregnancy until the very end."

"I'll probably stick to plain eggs from now on." She managed a wan smile.

"No, I'll cook breakfast," he said quickly. "Being ill like that can't be good for my children."

She leaned her head against his shoulder. "I always think I can keep going and going and never slow down. That's the first time I've been nauseated."

"Ugh, don't do it again," Zach said, his voice sympathetic. "I could cut fruit for breakfast."

"Fruit is my favorite," she said.

"Are you all right now?"

"I'm fine. Thank you."

An awkward moment passed between them. He desperately wanted to comfort her, and hold her, tell her she looked beautiful, tell her he was so excited that she was having his children—but he didn't know how she'd take that. He'd always heard pregnant women needed to be treated with care—that they could be *moody*. He wanted to avoid an argument. "Thank you for breakfast. Next time, my turn."

She smiled, relieved. "I plan to take you up on that."

"So, maybe dinner could be your thing. Something light. And I'll make you Pop-Tarts for breakfast. Or doughnuts. Fruit. Bagels. No cooking smells, maybe."

She nodded.

"All right," he said, glad they'd settled that for the moment. "I'm going out for a while."

"So am I."

He wanted to ask her where. His heart began pounding with concern, and he had to tell himself that they'd made an agreement and she would stick to it. "Let me know if you need anything," he said, heading outside.

He was living for the day when he could kiss her goodbye, like he wanted to do so badly. Although if he had his way, the goodbye kiss would last forever and move from the hallway to the bedroom.

I'm starting to scare myself.

"I've got to go see the council of elders," Zach said to himself. "I definitely need help on many levels."

Jessie tidied up, slightly embarrassed that she'd gotten ill in front of Zach. That's what she got for showing off, trying to be the good guest, the good wife-in-trial. She'd known her stomach had been queasy but put it down to wedding nerves. Relationship nerves.

It had definitely not been a Jessie's Girl Stuff-ready moment. For a woman used to making everything beautiful, she'd certainly been making messes.

Zach didn't seem to mind.

"I need help with this," she told herself, "before I make the biggest mess of my life." Packing her carpetbag, she left the house and hopped in her T-bird.

Twenty minutes later she was peeking through the windows of the Tulips Saloon. Shocked, she saw Zach was inside, talking to a woman she'd never seen. Having tea.

Backing away from the window, her heart pounding, she got back in her car, glancing around to make certain no one had seen her spying through the glass. She was chilled, and it wasn't because of the cold air blowing through the square. *Decorations,* she thought randomly, *the square would look so much better with Christmas decorations.*

"Stop," she said to herself. No more prettying things up. No more faking it. No more smiling when she felt sad or worried.

She got out of the car and walked inside the saloon.

Zach's face broke into a smile when he saw her. "Jessie, come meet Valentine Jefferson."

Jessie moved forward, putting a smile on her face.

"This is my wife, Jessie Forrester," Zach said,

and Jessie's skin jumped. Forrester. She'd almost forgotten.

"It's so nice to meet you," Valentine said. "I've heard so much about you, I feel as though you're my sister."

Jessie relaxed, and gave her a genuine smile. "Thank you."

"So you caught him," Valentine said. "Actually, I know better than that. The Forrester men remind me of the Jefferson boys in Union Junction. *He* caught *you*."

"I did," Zach said, "and I'm keeping her, too."

Valentine smiled. "I can't believe Pansy and Helen let you get away with an elopement."

"That's what elopements are for," Zach said happily. "Not asking anyone's permission and getting the deed done quick."

Jessie blinked. "It's nice to meet you, Valentine. I'm looking for Helen and Pansy, actually."

"They're in the kitchen." Zach leaned back. "Valentine brought a load of new cookies over for them to try, and they're inspecting her wares."

"I will, too, then. Sounds delicious." She smiled at Valentine and walked into the kitchen, trying not to panic at the thought of Zach talking to the beautiful redhead.

Pansy and Helen rushed over to hug her. "Congratulations!" Pansy said, while Helen said, "You're a daughter of Tulips now!"

"You look beautiful," Pansy said, and Helen said, "Glowing," and they began talking all at once so that nothing was really reaching Jessie except their happiness. She let herself bask in it for a moment before saying, "I need help."

They stopped chattering instantly.

"Anything," Helen said, and Pansy nodded.

"You two are the only ones I can ask," Jessie said. "I need to save my marriage. Before I totally screw it up."

Chapter Fourteen

Helen, Pansy and Jessie sat down at a small table in the kitchen. "I would have voted you Most Likely To Succeed, Jessie," Helen said. "Zach seems very happy to me."

Pansy nodded.

"It's the babies," she said. "I think our marriage should probably be based on more than that to make him happy. And I'm kind of nervous. I don't really know him."

"No, you don't," Pansy said. "But you have to understand, Zach can't stand to be bored. What you two did is something he relishes. It's that different-from-my-brother thing that makes him feel like a maverick."

"Not to mention he tied you down in one," Helen said practically. "Duke had to go to the altar twice to win Liberty. That probably feels very good to Zach."

Jessie took a deep breath. "We have fundamental differences, and I've always known that even makeup required a good foundation or everything on top cracked."

Helen nodded. "You're savvy, I'll give you that."

"Men do thrive on effort of the right sort," Pansy agreed. "We're not exactly short on answers, believe it or not. We do have more in our arsenal besides platitudes."

"True," Helen said. "Let me look through the recipe box." She dusted some flour off an old recipe box, and Jessie shook her head.

"I threw up when I cooked for Zach this morning. I was trying to be so…housewifey or something, and I cooked and then sort of ruined the effect," Jessie said miserably. "It's embarrassing to throw up on your first day as a newlywed."

Pansy and Helen stared at her over their spectacles. Then they glanced at each other before looking back at Jessie.

"No more cooking, dear," Helen said. "Men aren't good with moments of female gastric distress."

"Yes." Pansy nodded her head. "They want to believe we're always dainty, bouncy and ready to hop naked into a bed, stream or back seat, which-ever place they happen to be at the moment the call of the wild hits them."

Helen and Jessie gazed at Pansy in silence.

"Well," Helen said, "let's just stick with you not cooking anymore for a while." She closed the recipe box. "We're going to need a little time to work on this, Jessie, but we promise we know how to help you. Don't worry about a thing."

"Yes. Although we gave up on giving advice a long time ago, we may have a recipe that's appro-priate for your situation."

Jessie stood. "Thank you for listening. I feel better already."

Pansy and Helen hugged her goodbye. "Don't worry about a thing. We're just glad you're part of our town now."

Jessie left the kitchen, truly feeling better. Zach passed her on the way into the kitchen.

"I'm going to snatch one of those fresh cookies," he said.

She replied, "They're delicious, see you later," and kept on walking until she reached her car and drove away without anybody seeing the worry in her eyes.

She didn't need a recipe. For the first time in her

life, she needed a map—one that would point her in the direction of lasting love.

"Cookies," Zach said, walking into the kitchen. "Be still my heart."

Pansy smiled at him. "Your heart has always been drawn to sweet things."

"Jessie's pretty sweet," Helen said, and Zach nodded.

"She's a honey," he agreed, "and I just want to—"

"Congratulations again on your wedding," Helen said quickly. "I'm sure you were a handsome groom."

Zach shook his head, biting into a powdered chocolate crinkle. "Mmm. That is so good! I love Christmas. There's no time of year that the cooking is better." He gazed with delight over the trays of frosted reindeers, painted snowmen and sugared trees. "Are we having chocolate pecans this year? Or fudge?"

Helen began placing red hots on gingerbread men for buttons. "Just be glad for what we've got."

"Speaking of what we've got, Jessie had an awesome idea for a catch-and-release for men." Zach licked his fingers. "I think that's what she called it."

Helen looked at him. "Jessie thinks a lot, doesn't she? I don't believe I would have guessed she was a thinker when I first met her, but she really is."

"Yep," Zach said proudly. "Just when you think she's not thinking, she comes up with something I can't believe she'd think."

"Try to say that again," Pansy murmured, "if you *think* you can." She giggled.

"Okay," Zach said, settling into a chair, "so I was bragging a bit about her. But she's really special."

They smiled at him.

"Actually, I didn't come in here just to snitch cookies." Rubbing his chin, he pondered how to approach his two best Dear Abbys. "You know, Mom and Dad were happily married."

They nodded.

"Very stable. Real good parents. I want that for my kids, and for Jessie and me," he said. "But Jessie and I started our relationship so fast that now we're trying to slow it down, and it feels unnatural. I keep thinking Mom and Dad didn't seem to have any speeds, just an even keel of harmony and love and respect."

"Well," Helen said, "they were of similar backgrounds and goals."

"Yeah," Zach said, "I know the scales on my marriage are tipped toward short, and I want them to weigh in more toward long-term."

"I have to admit I didn't think Jessie was right for you in the beginning," Helen said. "She has certainly proven herself to be a wonderful young woman that Tulips can be proud to call its own."

"Yes. You were lucky," Pansy said, "in spite of her hitting poor Brahma Bud."

"Oh, Bud," Zach said. "She barely tapped him, and he barely noticed. How hard she's hit me is a whole other story, though."

Helen and Pansy gazed at him for a long time, gentle smiles on their faces.

"This from a western romance writer," Helen said with a sweet smile. "I thought you'd have all the answers."

Zach stared at his two dearest friends. "How'd you know?"

They giggled. "While you were gone with Jessie, two beautiful women stopped in on the way to your house. Naturally, we inquired."

"I'm afraid they told us your secret," Pansy said, not sorry at all, "and they left us something to give you." She pulled out a brown envelope. "We've been waiting for you to return so we could ask your permission to read it," she said hopefully.

"You haven't already?" he asked.

"Of course not!" Pansy exclaimed. "We're not busybodies!"

Zach laughed. "Tell you what—you can read my work-in-progress if you help me win Jessie for good. I really want her to be happy, and I sincerely do not want to screw this up."

"Now where have I heard that?" Helen asked, looking at Pansy with a grin.

"We'll need time to think about it," Pansy said. "Our best ideas come to us over tea." She put his manuscript in the drawer. "Although we don't think you need us. Any man brave enough to write a book is brave enough to win a woman's heart."

"But I want Jessie's," Zach said, "and that's a puzzle."

"We like puzzles," Helen said. "We'll get right on it."

They gave him a gentle shove toward the door, so Zach grabbed a couple of snowmen and reindeer and left the saloon.

It was Christmas, for Pete's sake. Surely there was one miracle with his name written on it.

Chapter Fifteen

That night Jessie walked into the barn to look for Zach. As much as it felt like Tulips was her home now, she and Zach had agreed to divorce following the babies' birth, and she had an international company to run.

She supposed she could always move her offices here, and she was essentially on break for the holidays. There would be plenty of time to look for a house.

Yet, she wondered if she'd ever really be a town girl at heart.

The air inside the barn was hazy, a strange type of smoky. Jessie held her breath, not wanting to breathe the smell. "Zach?"

"Back here," he called.

Some of the alarm ebbed out of her system at

the sound of his voice. "I didn't know if something was on fire or someone was smoking pot. It smells terrible."

Zach turned around. He'd been soothing a horse as another man worked on its hooves. "Pot? Does it smell like pot?"

"Well, pretty much," Jessie said. "I'm sure it's not healthy to breathe for long."

"It's the farrier. He's trimming the horses' hooves. It's got to be done every once in a while." Zach squinted at her through the dusty acridness. "Never thought about the smell of it before."

"Yeesh," Jessie said. "It doesn't quite have the aroma of Pansy's and Helen's bakery."

"You're right." Zach took her arm and walked her from the barn. "I forget what a sensitive city critter you are."

"I'm not!" she exclaimed, tugging her arm away. "Anybody would say that hoof business is stinky—you're just being stubborn."

"Calm down," he said calmly, rubbing her back. "All that upset isn't good for my babies. Not to mention they shouldn't know that their mother knows anything about marijuana."

"I don't personally," Jessie said, annoyed. "It's just there are some things one comes across at parties and concerts. But I wouldn't know it if I saw it."

"Well, I do," Zach said as he pulled Jessie down into his lap on a bench outside the barn. "Duke, Holt, Liberty and I got some weed from a high school friend who was growing it in his back forty where his parents wouldn't find his plants. We thought we were so cool, sneaking a smoke out where no one could see us, nothing around us but blue sky and dry grass. Liberty couldn't smoke worth a damn, and truthfully, I don't think she tried very hard. Holt had a coughing fit, and he didn't get more than a puff. Me and Duke, though, had to show off and act like we could smoke when we couldn't, and we ended up blowing out more than we took in. You wouldn't have thought being outdoors the smoke would cling to our clothes, but it did, and Mom smelled it."

"Uh-oh," Jessie said. "How'd she know what it was?"

Zach smiled at the memory. "Mom wasn't interested in what kind of smoke it was. It was smoke, and her kids had been out doing it, and we got the hidin' of our lives from Dad. Later on, the whole story came out, since Holt went home so sick. His parents told mine what we'd really been doing, and the folks grounded us off riding for three months. We also had to paint every building in the town square a fresh coat of paint over our summer vacation. That was a hardship," Zach said, shaking his head. "No swimming in the pond, no vacation, no nothing. Just paint, paint and more paint. Mom said if we wanted to be around stuff that would make our brains funny, we could get funny and do some good at the same time."

"Wow. I would have liked your mom," Jessie said.

He nodded. "If I'd known you then, I wouldn't have gotten in as much trouble, though."

She crooked her brow. "Why?"

"I would have known to say that the farrier had been out where I'd been, and that's what the smell was." He ran a hand through her long hair. "I wish I'd known you then, Jessie T."

"No," Jessie said. "Lying to your mother would have made you a dishonest person. Remember, you're already known to make a situation suit you when necessary."

"Now, Jessie," he said, "you've got to quit being mad about that. Not to mention, you're the one who makes ugly things pretty. Is that lying to a man if a woman's beauty comes out of a bottle? Isn't that trickery? The poor fellow thinks he's getting a show horse, then one night, he surprises his lady in the bathroom and discovers what he really got was a rack pony."

Jessie slapped him on the hand. "You're supposed to see my inner goodness no matter what."

"I do," he said. "I don't like the fakery and tricks women weave."

"*Pfft.* Zach Forrester, when some men say it's raining, a woman has to look outside to see if he's telling the truth."

Getting up, he tugged her toward the house.

"What are you doing?"

"I'm taking you inside and giving you a spanking," Zach said.

She pulled back. "Like hell."

He laughed. "I'm teasing. It's time to make your dinner. I can tell you get upset on an empty stomach, and I don't want my children going hungry."

"Stop." She dug in her heels so that their hands slipped apart. "Zach, I'm sorry, but it's either me or the children, as strange as that sounds."

A frown hovered on his handsome face. "Meaning?"

"You can't romance all three of us. We're not a family yet, and I...I need to feel like you and I have something in common besides parenthood."

He blinked. "We have nothing in common."

Ouch. "Okay. Then we need to find something. Before the children are born. Otherwise, I'm going to feel like one of your—" She stretched a hand out to encompass the barns and fields. "I don't know the proper word for female mother horse."

"Mare."

She looked at him, her hands on her hips. For the first time, she realized how important it was that they had some kind of connection that went beyond their pregnancy.

He stepped toward her, his eyes suddenly dark with a look she'd never seen before. "Zach?"

He kissed her slow and hot, his hands framing her face as he completely possessed her lips. Her soul seemed to melt inside her. Everything up to that moment between them had been fun and light-hearted. But not this kiss. He went for her heart and her fears and her secrets, and when he finally broke away from her to stare down into her eyes, Jessie had very little reserves left to challenge him.

"You," he said. "It's you."

Her fingers went to her lips, unconsciously touching the skin he'd set on fire.

"I'm done," the farrier called. "Is that the last one, or have you got more in the field?"

Zach gave her one last, silent look before striding toward the barns. Shaken, Jessie went inside the house, torn between happiness and being nervous. She'd never felt any of this with the man she might have married, and it was confusing that she hadn't.

She might have married a man who didn't make her knees tremble and her heart beat crazily fast. Was it a good sign that a man could make her feel this way with one kiss—or were her parents correct in believing that she'd lost her normal good common sense?

On the kitchen counter lay two pieces of mail: one, a brown envelope addressed to Zach in a flowing script. It appeared to have no postage. The other was a FedEx envelope addressed to her. She recognized Fran's handwriting on the label.

Wondering what business her secretary and best friend might have needed to forward to her that she couldn't have called her about, Jessie tore open the mailer. Inside was a white envelope addressed in her father's strong handwriting. She tore that open, finding a letter and an official document.

Jessie,
We know you're on your honeymoon or we would have called you about this, and yet a

simple phone call would not have sufficed. Given the circumstances of your recent decision to wed someone unknown to the family and our business associates, we feel it is best to terminate your position at Jessie's Girl Stuff and Farnsworth Enterprises. You will always be our daughter, but in the years to come, we are certain you will thank us for protecting you from your impetuous and, we feel, rash decision. Your mother, brothers and I are very sorry about this rift that has come into our relationship, but we know that one day the Jessie we know will return to us.

Dad

The accompanying document underlined her father's words in legal terms she knew the family lawyers had carefully chosen. Hot tears of devastated pain jumped into her eyes.

Zach walked in and she turned away so he wouldn't see her anguish, taking the envelope with her as she went to her room. She put it in a drawer, closing it tightly, putting off the shock until she could absorb it later.

"Hey," Zach said, knocking on her door. "You all right in there?"

No. "I'm fine."

He was silent for a moment. "Jessie, please open the door."

It was his house. Jessie waited for him to open the door himself, doing as he pleased in typical Zach fashion. But he didn't, and she realized she was holding her breath.

She swung the door open. "Yes?"

He gazed at her. "You've been crying, and I upset you. I'm sorry. I shouldn't have kissed you. It went beyond the boundaries of our agreement. I promise not to make you feel uncomfortable again."

He turned and walked away.

She wanted to go after him, to tell him that he'd misunderstood the source of her unhappiness and that with him, she was finally beginning to understand what she'd been needing in her life.

She went into the hall but he was gone, and he hadn't taken his envelope with him. It was a good excuse to go upstairs and see him, she told herself, egging her bravery to come forth. Picking up the large brown envelope, she put her foot on the stairs, wondering if she could take her first steps to going upstairs to the part of the house she never had set foot in.

Was it smart to cross a boundary they'd both agreed on?

She wasn't sure. It was too early in their marriage to know. She didn't want to shatter anything precious that might have built between them. Glancing down at the envelope, she told herself she didn't need an excuse to talk to him—she was married to him. Playing mail carrier wasn't the answer; strength of purpose was.

A note on the back of the envelope caught her eye.

Wonderful, wonderful, we knew you could do it. We just about rode off with the hero ourselves.
Love, Helen and Pansy

Zach's secret manuscript. This was precious, then, and certainly worth a trip upstairs, where she could apologize and then share the news she still couldn't take in. Zach was the perfect person to talk to. He understood family issues. He wouldn't get overwrought about it; he wouldn't offer advice she couldn't use. He'd simply listen—and Jessie realized that was a valuable commodity she liked in him. He simply never judged her. Teased her, yes, but never judged her.

It was sneaky, but she was dying to take just one peep inside the creative side of the strong man she barely knew. Just one small look, as Helen and Pansy and "The Twins" had gotten. Surely something he meant for publication wasn't a secret from his wife...his temporary wife.

Jessie slipped the front page from the envelope, her eyes scanning hungrily.

Bronson James would never have married the woman beside him if he hadn't known she was a gunslinger's daughter. The gunslinger's reputation needed no bragging. His daughter's reputation needed polishing. Bronson didn't give a damn either way because he'd married her for money, for protection and for the babies he intended to put in her belly. On the untamed prairie, there wasn't a better deal to be made than the one he'd just let the circuit preacher seal. The bitter fruits of bad decisions had brought him to this point of no return, but he wouldn't have turned back anyway. Not now. A man of conviction never retraced his bootsteps lest he know himself as a coward, and Bronson James was no godforsaken coward.

Jessie gasped. Her fingers trembling, she shoved the page back in. Glancing upstairs to make certain she hadn't been seen, she left the stairwell and hurried over to the entry table, returning the envelope to its place. Her heart thundered inside her chest.

Wild, hurt thoughts whirled inside her. She was in a strange place with few acquaintances and no Fran to discuss her sudden fears with. She didn't even have a company anymore. Her family had chosen to show their disapproval of her actions by voting her out of the company, which hurt more than she could have imagined. She didn't know her husband.

She jumped in her car and drove off the ranch.

Chapter Sixteen

"I liked Jessie's ideas," Pansy said. "She's got a quick brain."

Helen nodded. "How about a June fish catch-n-fry?"

"I like it," Pansy said. "June is for summer lovers, you know. If we're going to pick a month to throw out our lures, we might as well pick one with positive portent!" She giggled and sipped some tea.

"We just need to put the idea forward to the menfolk," Helen said.

"Duke," Pansy finished the thought.

"Don't forget Rocky and Bullwinkle." Helen sniffed.

"Oh, Hiram and Bug will be more than glad to help."

Helen sat up. "Where are we going to get bait?"

"Victoria's Secret," Pansy said blithely. "Our girls will figure that out, don't worry. And we'll be here for advice, and Liberty, too. That girl knows a little something about lace."

"I meant fish bait," Helen said.

"Oh," Pansy said. "Who cares about that? If the men are thinking about bait out in those boats with our girls, then we haven't done our job!"

"I like the way you think." Helen laid cookie tins on the table. "Valentine brought these by. She thought we could use a new look for Christmas in our cookie design."

"She's so talented," Pansy said, lifting up a decorated Christmas cookie shaped like a tulip. Illustrations were included with each new tin, so that they could see how to frost tiny tulips on tree branches, and even on snowman bellies.

A knock on Helen's front door startled them. "Must be the guys," Helen said, getting up. "It's always high-tea time around here for Bug and Hiram, and they have no qualms about hunting cookies."

She opened to door, surprised to see Jessie outside. "How lovely to see you, dear," she said, hugging her. "Pansy and I were just talking about you."

Jessie walked inside the softly lit foyer, breathing in the comforting aroma of baking. "I saw your tree was lit from outside," she said. "I hope you don't mind me stopping by this late without calling."

"I'd be upset if you didn't." Helen nodded at her tree. "Pansy and I just finished putting on the last touches."

"It's beautiful," Jessie said. Zach's tree still had nothing but candy canes on it. She'd meant to help him finish it, but now... Lovely sparkling lights of many colors lit Helen's tree, and silver balls hung from every branch. A pink tulip garnished the top, and filmy pink ribbons cascaded down the sides. She realized she'd always been traveling right before Christmas and had never put up a tree in her Dallas loft.

There were things in her life she'd sacrificed for her job, and now she wondered why. "I've always been on the go," she murmured.

"Yes," Helen said, nodding. "You're so talented and smart to get as far as you have in life."

"There's more to life than the corporate ladder. It's a lesson I've just begun to learn," Jessie said.

"Twins. You'll be surprised how your ladder is going to change from corporate to angelic. Come in the kitchen. We were hoping to see you soon because we have something for you. We just didn't want to bother you and Zach on your honeymoon."

Pansy enveloped Jessie in a tight embrace. "So good to see you. We've been trying to give you some time to settle in with your new husband."

Jessie looked at the tiny china plate Helen put before her, with a matching teacup. "I always feel so much better when I'm with you two."

"Now that doesn't sound like the voice of a honeymooner. Not to pry," Pansy said, "but is something wrong?"

It felt like she melted. Jessie told her friends about her parents' letter and reading Zach's book—which she shouldn't have done—and, worst of all, the tension between them. She told it without tears, but the tears stayed locked inside her like cold stones. "It hurts," she said, "more than anything in my life. I'm not sure how one day I was going down the road freestyle, and now my life is completely out of whack."

"Changes," Pansy said.

"But I always adapt so well. I like change."

"It's the people around you who are having to change, and they're not adapting well," Helen said. "Let us give you a wedding gift."

"Just a recipe," Pansy told her, "but it's worked for someone once. It may again."

Jessie took the slim light pink envelope. "Can I read it?"

"Not now." Helen smiled. "It's meant to be read in private, when you have time to sit and think about what you really want and what's most important to you."

"Thank you." Jessie tucked the envelope into her carpetbag. "I can't wait."

"This is all going to work out," Helen said. "The babies are the most important thing. You need to make certain you're getting good prenatal care, and take care of yourself. Think happy thoughts. Eat well. The rest will fall into place eventually if you focus on your children." She smiled at her. "You are happy about your babies, aren't you?"

"I'm thrilled beyond words." Jessie smiled, feeling the glow of happiness radiating inside her just thinking about the two babies she would one day hold. "It's more than I ever dreamed of."

"Well, then," Pansy said, "you just think about that, because they're all that matters besides your man, of course. But you have a recipe for that." She winked at her. "Now, dear, help us a little more with this idea of yours for a catch-n-release party.

We need to catch as many tourists of high quality as possible."

"I can take care of that," Jessie said. "Since I'm no longer employed by my family, I can use my client base to send out invitations. I couldn't have before, because of conflict, but now I can."

Pansy blinked. "How many?"

"Selectively, I have a client base of several thousand around the world. We could start small and focused, perhaps just the Texas corporations I deal with for our first year. This will be the time to figure out our mistakes and what we'd do different next year."

"Oh, my," Helen said, "we'd best get busy."

"How are you going to do this and concentrate on your children?" Pansy asked.

Jessie laughed, delighted just to be included in their dreams. "My babies won't be born for several months. I'll work on the invitations, and you marshal your troops. We'll need lots of volunteers come June."

Helen smiled. "We're so very glad you've come to Tulips, Jessie. You're just what we've been needing."

Jessie smiled. Maybe she would stay here in Tulips—whether or not she and Zach worked matters out. It was beginning to feel a lot like a real home to her, and her children would benefit from what they could learn from people with such good hearts.

"Christmas is such a wonderful time of year," she said, and Helen and Pansy beamed. "I never slowed down enough to enjoy it before."

She hoped Zach would be happy to know that Tulips was working its spell on her. "I'm going home now," she said.

Pansy and Helen looked at her.

"To the ranch," she clarified.

They just smiled.

ZACH WAS beside himself when he realized Jessie had left. His worst nightmare washed over him. What if she didn't come back?

She would. She had to.

He'd not really given her a reason to.

She will. She has to. I want her to.

Her bedroom door was open, so he walked in, looking around. She kept everything neat: the bed, the closet, her things on the dresser. The room smelled of Jessie, a light peachy fragrance he loved. He touched a lipstick she'd left out, picking it up. *Jessie's Girl Stuff.*

She was girly, but she was also strong.

He left the room, closing the door behind him. There was nothing to do but wait, and hope he got a chance to apologize.

Going into the living room, he sat across from the Christmas tree. The candy canes seemed lonely and lost in the branches, so he tried to envision the day when, not only would the tree be covered with glittering ornaments and perhaps a shiny star on top, but loads of presents for little children would lay gaily wrapped in paper underneath.

Goose bumps ran over his arms at the thought.

It wouldn't be Christmas without Jessie. Surely she'd just run to the store, the saloon, somewhere close by.

The phone rang, and he leaped for it. "Hello?"

"Zach, it's Pepper."

"Oh," he said.

"And a very merry, scintillating, overexuberant Christmas season to you, too," she said. "Heard you got married on the sly."

"I did." He sank back onto the sofa, staring miserably at the unadorned tree. "Where the hell are you?"

"Up with Aunt Jerry. She gets lonely this time of year."

"Yeah, me, too."

"You can't be lonely. You have a wife."

He snapped out of his piteous mood. "I meant I might have been lonely."

"But now you have Jessie."

Not really. "Exactly."

"Congratulations," she said. "I wouldn't have thought you'd be the Forrester to elope."

"Yeah, it could've been you."

She was silent.

"Well, I mean, if you had someone you wanted to marry," he said quickly, not wanting to hurt his sister's feelings.

She sighed. "Zach, take good care of Jessie, okay?"

He frowned. "Is something wrong?"

"No, and yes," she said. "Someday, I'm going to tell you something I should have told you a long time ago."

"Yeesh," he said. "You're not coming back to town?"

"Oh, I'm coming back. I've bought a building for my clinic and a place to live."

He relaxed. "Good. I've gotten used to you being around. Sometimes I even miss you, as much as I shouldn't swell your head by telling you."

"We have a lot in common. Merry Christmas, Zach," she said, hanging up the phone before he could say the same. He stared at the phone in his hand for a moment before clicking it off. "Women are so moody," he said, going back to thinking about how gloomy the house would be if Jessie hadn't ever hit Brahma Bud.

It seemed so long ago.

But he'd caught her, for the moment. He paced to the window, staring out in the darkness, looking for headlights. Turning to consider the tree, he thought about occupying his time by getting out a box of ornaments. The thought depressed him, and he decided he was being moody like Pepper, and Forresters shouldn't all be moody at the same time, so he got out some M&M's and amused himself for a moment by tossing them in the air and catching them in his mouth.

The challenge of that only lasted a moment before he realized he hadn't been bored since Jessie had come into his life. She was what he'd needed all along. "Come home," he said aloud. "I swear, I'll follow Prince Charming's blueprint and sweep you off your feet."

He couldn't take thinking about it anymore so

he put himself to bed. In the morning, he was going to go throw himself on the little ladies for help.

ZACH GOT UP the next morning to start his chores, nearly kicking his heels up with joy at seeing the T-bird parked in its spot. His whole mood improved instantly.

Unable to bear not seeing her, he went and tapped on her bedroom door. There was no answer, so he gingerly pushed it open.

She slept soundly, her arms curled around a pillow. *That should be me she's holding. I'm doing something wrong if a pillow is my substitute.*

Maybe that was the way she liked to sleep. Silently, he closed the door. "Either way it should be me in that bed with her," he said, hurrying outside to feed the animals and do his chores.

Then he cleaned up and left, determined to get some advice from the only people who could help him.

"Not that I'm helpless," he said, when Helen opened the door to let him in, "but this one matters to me and I'm kind of messing things up."

"You mean Jessie?" Helen asked with twinkling eyes.

"Well, yes, ma'am." He entered as she indicated and gave her a kiss on the cheek. "Where's your comrade?"

"In the kitchen trying to place decorations on sugar-cookie trees. It's not easy with her macular degeneration," Helen said. "The eyes play a few tricks on her."

"It's not getting worse, is it?"

"No," Helen said, "but it's dicey, of course."

His heartbeat slowed a bit. If there was one thing he wanted more than anything else in the world—besides Jessie and healthy babies—he wanted these two women and Hiram and Bug to see his children's faces. These four people had been his parents ever since his own had passed away, and through them he still had a connection to the warm love his family had given him and Pepper and Duke.

He walked into the kitchen and surprised Pansy with a big hug. "You're beautiful," he told her.

"Gosh," Helen said good-naturedly. "You've never told me that."

He winked at her. "I'll tell you again when you get me a glass of milk to go with my cookies."

She lightly rapped his knuckles with a wooden spoon, so he sat back, enjoying the smells of cinnamon and ginger. "Please teach me what I'm lacking," he said as Helen put a delicate plate of cookies within his reach. "I know you know."

Pansy stopped. "Oh, you made me draw a crooked line of dots."

"Maybe you should rest your eyes," Helen said and Pansy glared at her.

"Maybe I just need quiet to be creative," she said. "All artists work better that way."

"Tea…to soothe the savage beast," Helen said, and went to prepare a breakfast blend for her friend.

Pansy winked mischievously at Zach. "She fell for it. Jessie stopped by here last night, by the way."

He sat up to listen, Jessie being his favorite topic. "I wondered where she went. I didn't think about her coming over here." He'd been afraid she'd simply left town.

"Communication is the key," Helen said. "Jessie had gotten some bad news. She feels adrift right now and that's understandable."

"She's got me," Zach said, but Pansy shook her head.

"Does she?" Pansy asked. "She has to know that for herself."

"Maybe she doesn't know it yet, but surely she'll be able to figure that out in time," he said.

Helen shook her head. "Why do men never want to talk about their feelings?"

"Because we're afraid we'll insult the woman, or have our emotions left to dry in the wind when the woman rejects us. Those are the scenarios which keep a man's mouth closed." In his case, perhaps both fears were in play. He was walking on eggshells around Jessie, trying to keep to their agreement, and he was afraid she might decide he wasn't the man for her. "I guess I'm talking about men in general. My fear is that Jessie will decide she doesn't want to continue our marriage. I may not be able to convince her."

"Go see her," Helen said. "Talk it over."

"Do you love her, Zach?" Pansy asked.

"More than I ever thought possible," he replied. "It's hit me like a bat between the eyes."

The ladies giggled.

"We waited a long time to hear that," Helen said. "Now we have a little something for you." She handed him an envelope with his name on it and shooed him to the door. "Come back anytime. But right now, go home."

"That's good advice," he said, adjusting his hat for courage.

"Of course it is," Pansy said, letting him give her a peck on the cheek. "We've decided that's all we give."

ZACH WENT HOME feeling better but not in charge of the situation. Jessie's car was parked outside, so that instantly brightened his spirits.

But first perhaps he needed to read his letter, he decided. He needed a few tips on taming an heiress who didn't really need him. Pulling out the envelope, he impatiently tore it open.

A Recipe For Winning Your Sweetly
Stubborn Wife

Be Kind. Marriages are built on kindness and respect. Talk about pretty things and the future you will share together.

Be Thoughtful—as you are. Old movies and garden-picked flowers will show her your romantic side.

Call her parents and invite them to the ranch. Wealthy social people have feelings, too, that they don't know what to do with. As afraid as they are of losing their wealth, they're afraid of losing Jessie more.

He blinked. "Damn hard recipe," he murmured. But he had nothing to lose in trying. For Jessie, he would try anything, even if he was pretty sure the little old ladies were wrong about this recipe.

JESSIE PULLED OUT the pink envelope Helen and Pansy had given her, opening it eagerly in the privacy of her room.

How To Win Your Handsome, Slightly
Chauvinistic Husband Who Doesn't
Show His Feelings

Be patient. True love is experienced once, maybe twice in a lifetime. It's not like baking cookies with a recipe that comes out the same every time if you use the right ingredients. Zach hasn't experienced the ingredients before.

Be honest. He loves real and true things. Hiding feelings just hurts you both.

Remember what drew you both together and try a little more of that.

Call your parents. They love you. It's hard to go forward when you haven't made peace with the past—even if they're the instigators. They're used to having you all to themselves.

Jessie shook her head. There was more to following one of the Gang's recipes than she'd anticipated. But where Zach was concerned, it was worth a shot.

She shrieked when he tapped on her door. "Yes?"

"Can I bother you for a second?"

Her heart began a restless racing at the sound of his voice. She opened the door, overjoyed to see him. "You're not bothering me."

He removed his hat, and handed her a candy cane he'd put foil on to look like a flower. "Sorry. Garden flowers are out of season right now. Best I could do."

She smiled at him. "I didn't know you were so talented."

He nodded. "Neither did I. It was a stretch."

Putting the flower on her dresser she said, "I got a letter from my parents removing me from my position at the company."

"Whoa," he said. "Jessie, I'm sorry."

She shrugged, not wanting him to know how badly she was hurt. "They had their reasons."

"Yeah. Me."

"Which I don't agree with." She lifted her chin. "I'd rather have these children than the company."

She almost said, "You and these children than

the company," but stopped herself in time. Helen and Pansy hadn't said, *Throw yourself at him and see if he catches you.*

"You really are happy about the pregnancy, aren't you?" he asked.

"I've always wanted children. I just wouldn't have gotten them with my ex, which I now realize. It's ironic to me that I might have married him and had nothing, and I wasn't married to you and was given so much."

He shifted in the doorway. "I'm glad you're here," he said gruffly.

"I'm glad to be here," she said, meaning it.

"Even though you won't be spending Christmas with your folks?"

"I feel that they made their decisions. I'd rather be where I'm wanted."

His jaw tensed for a moment. "You're wanted."

They looked at each other for a long moment before he stepped inside the doorway and took her in his arms. "I know we agreed on temporary, but I'm pretty sure this won't be going away anytime soon," he said, kissing her, and Jessie's body sang an agreement her mouth was too busy to say.

They fell onto the bed together, reaching for each other's clothes at the same time. If her friends hadn't reminded her that what had brought them together was good and important, she might not be able to lose herself in the magic of this moment. She unbuttoned his shirt with speed equal to his as he undressed her, and then they lay in each other's arms, naked to each other for the first time.

"God, you're beautiful," he said. "I know that sounds like something any guy would say when he's about to score, but Jessie, you're beyond my wildest imaginings."

His hard body stirred her longings as well, and Jessie fought back the shyness to express herself by touching him first on the chest, and then lower, stroking and guiding him to her. "I was wondering if I'd imagined the way we felt together."

"No," Zach said, moving into her, "you didn't. It was good then," he murmured against her lips, "and it's going to be better now."

He carefully and gently rocked her to an incredible climax, and held her close when she cried out with pleasure as he shuddered with his own excitement. "Too fast," he complained. "I'm probably always going to be too fast with you. You get me the way I never expected to want a woman."

They lay in each other's arms, quietly enjoying the intimacy growing between them.

"I believe all good things happen for a reason," Zach murmured against her hair, and she nodded. She did, too. There was no other explanation for Brahma Bud to have stepped in her path, bringing her to meet her destiny.

"I called your parents," Zach murmured, and the cocoon of safety and joy was ripped from her.

She sat up and looked at him. "Why?"

He tried to pull her against him but she wouldn't unstiffen. "Because it's the holidays. Words were spoken in haste. I felt it was important to extend the olive branch."

She got out of bed and began dressing. "You conveniently didn't tell me that until after we'd made love. Zach, they fired me. Their only daughter."

"And I'm the cause of that." He reached to grab her arm. "Jessie, we're all family. And those babies need to know their grandparents."

"All the same," Jessie said, "in the future, please consider my feelings before you go off acting like Sam Houston fighting my battles."

Chapter Seventeen

Zach stared at his wife, confused. Pansy and Helen had specifically felt that he should make some effort toward her family, and though he'd rather not, he'd done it for Jessie. "Stop," he said. "You're not leaving this room." Getting up from the bed, he quickly dressed. Before she could get away from him, he reached out and grabbed her. "Oh, no, you don't, Jessie. You just ran out of run with me."

She let him hold her arm with a mutinous gleam in her eye.

"Now see, I've had horses look at me like that, and that's a sign to me that I haven't finished my work with you. You need me, beautiful, and I need you. So let's just take a deep breath together and talk this out."

"I don't need anyone's help with my family,"

Jessie said. "They're entitled to their feelings and I'm certainly entitled to mine. You have no right to butt into our private world."

He nodded. "It's like that, is it?"

"Yes! Of course it is!" She took a deep breath before saying, "Nowhere in our marriage contract did we agree to be anything more than temporary. And I certainly don't need you interfering with my corporate or family business."

For a long moment he stared at her, realizing that there were parts to him and Jessie that were wider than a gulf. He figured Helen and Pansy were right to encourage her family to come to his world, so whatever fears they had about him could be resolved. Resolution could only benefit Jessie and his children, he'd been certain.

Inviting her parents—and her brothers—to the ranch for Christmas hadn't been the easiest thing he'd ever done. But she didn't like the gift he was trying to give her. He shrugged. "Sorry. Next time I won't."

He left her room as a man who knew a little bit more about Jessie than he had five minutes before. She was serious about her space—and he was going to let her have all the space she could find.

It was a damn big ranch.

JESSIE REGRETTED the rush of angry words that came out of her mouth as soon as she said them, but it took her two days to find Zach so that she could somehow bridge the gap between them. He was in the attic, a place she would never have thought to look except that the ladder was down. For two days, he'd been a ghost, the only clue he was still in the house the smell of breakfast in the air, or coffee percolating in a pot with two mugs laid out beside it.

She climbed the ladder and poked her head through the opening. "Zach, can we talk?"

"I'm busy right now."

It was too close to Christmas to take no for an answer. Her parents' actions had made her angry and fearful and she'd taken it out on Zach. She'd needed a bit more time to assimilate how she felt about being pushed out of the family circle, but truthfully, it had made her realize all the more that Zach's family circle was the one she wanted: him, her and their two babies were a complete family. She stood before him, her heart anxious for forgiveness. "Zach, there've been a few times when you haven't let me run away from you, and this time you're not going to shut me out."

He glanced up, handing her a picture among

many he was looking at in a box. "Those are my parents. It's the closest you'll get to meeting them, I'm sorry to say."

She felt tears jump into her eyes. "Zach, thank you for trying to include my family in our lives. I should have told you that the other day. Instead, I spoke with the anger and bitterness that I was feeling for what they'd done. It's not the easiest thing that's ever happened to me, and I haven't taken it well."

"What they did was wrong, but it's their loss," Zach said. "But I don't want to come between you and your family forever. I figured Christmas was a time for forgiveness, and I still feel that way." He stood, looking down at her. "I feel bad that I'm the cause for this pain in your life, Jessie, and your family. I'd fix it if I could, but I can't."

There. Helen and Pansy would have to be proud of him for expressing how he felt. "I know this is our first challenge, but I have to say that I'm enjoying even this with you."

"Why?" she asked. "I'm afraid of disharmony."

He touched her cheek. "I'm not afraid of it if it means everyone understands each other better in the end."

"I don't know," Jessie whispered. "We have some very tough challenges facing us."

"As long as we make an addendum to our contract that says we always speak our minds and listen to each other, we'll just grow together, if that's what you want."

"I do," Jessie said softly, and Zach felt a piece of the wall between them crumble away. He ran a finger down a strand of her long hair, enjoying its silkiness.

"Never do we go to bed angry again," he told her, and Jessie nodded.

"In fact," she said, "it's high time you continue this theme of closeness in my bed every night."

He grinned. "You'll like my room better."

She looked at him. "Is that an invitation?"

Her face felt delicate between his palms as he cradled her. "You never needed an invitation."

Maybe she didn't, but that didn't mean she felt free to bridge that gap in their relationship. Especially not with the feelings she'd stored inside her from the words she'd read in his manuscript. "One day, then," she said, breaking away from him to scurry back down the stairs.

"Running?" he asked, watching her descent with a grin.

"It's important not to jump to conclusions," she

said, lifting her chin. "I'm merely leaving you to your cleaning."

He laughed, and Jessie decided to tackle a chore that she'd long wanted to finish. It was four days before Christmas and his tree was still barely decorated. The house seemed to be waiting, unnaturally empty of holiday spirit.

A box sat beside the tree, opened but not yet disturbed. Gently, Jessie took out an ornament, freezing when she saw the picture of Zach, Pepper and Duke as children set inside, all three of them dressed in matching candy-striped pajamas.

She had a picture like this of her and her brothers on her tree that by now Fran would have put up in her office. She gasped. "Fran!"

Running to grab her cell phone, she quickly dialed her best friend. "Fran, it's Jessie."

"And Merry Christmas to you, too," Fran said. "It's good to hear your voice. You've been a lot quieter since you caught that handsome cowboy. Congratulations on your decision to live forever in the sticks, by the way. I always said you worked too hard."

Jessie frowned. "What decision to live in the sticks?"

"Sorry," Fran said with a laugh, "I shouldn't

phrase it that way. Congratulations on your desire to make your home with your new husband and expected children."

"I didn't tell you that," she said, her blood running cold.

"I read it in the corporate memo. And also your parents mentioned your decision to me when they called to instruct me to forward to their corporate offices all documents pertaining to the job from which you'd resigned."

Jessie blinked back shock. "Corporate memo?"

"Yeah. Worldwide. All offices. Well, a position as big as yours would require an announcement to all offices, of course. It's not every day a Farnsworth gives up a prestigious family position."

She should have foreseen this, of course. "Lovely," she said, and Fran gasped.

"Don't tell me you didn't authorize this," Fran said.

"The company decided that it would be better in other hands in light of my unorthodox marriage," she said, the feelings of betrayal rising inside her again.

"Oh, Jessie, I'm so sorry."

"I don't understand it myself." Jessie shook her

head. "And yet, I somehow feel it's for the best. I'm certainly not losing on the trade-off."

"You're happy, then? In Tulips?"

Jessie hesitated, touching the picture ornament of Zach and his siblings she'd placed on the tree. "If you'd told me six months ago that I'd be without a job and living in the country, married to a cowboy and pregnant, I would have thought you were insane. Not in any way did this fit my plans for the future. But oddly enough, every day I change a little more, and it's all good."

"You're giving me shivers," she said. "I want that, too."

Jessie laughed. "But you still have a job."

"Actually, no," Fran said, her tone quiet. "Once I send the boxes of documents, I'm to close the office. Jessie, I promise I thought this was what you wanted."

Something snapped inside Jessie. At first she'd been embarrassed of how her family was acting. Then she worried Zach would feel cheated because he'd married a woman with few financial reserves at the moment, not to mention that he'd signed a prenup, guaranteeing his exclusion from any gains from their marriage.

But Fran deserved better. "First, I want you to

come to Tulips," Jessie said. "You're the most organized person I know. Come out here and find yourself a world of people who love newcomers."

"And employment?" Fran asked.

"Let's walk on the wild side," Jessie suggested. "Let's go into some kind of business for ourselves."

"Wow," Fran breathed, and Jessie nodded to herself. It was the right thing to do.

"What about Zach? Will he mind you starting a new venture?"

"No," Jessie said, "my man will applaud me for not buckling to pressure."

"Then I'll pack this office as fast as I can and head your way. Jessie, you're the best friend I ever had."

Jessie smiled, and hanging up, went back upstairs to the attic to talk to her husband. "Zach?"

"Yes." He swept a bunch of cobwebs from the eaves with a broom. "This hasn't been cleaned up here in years."

"I can see that," she said. "Is there a reason you're doing it right before Christmas and not, say, in the spring?"

"Hell if I know," Zach said, and Jessie nodded.

"Perhaps there's hidden meanings we should consider."

"I doubt it. I think the attic just needs a good cleaning."

"Zach," Jessie said, "I read a page of your manuscript."

He quit sweeping and put the broom down. "Payback for hiding your car?"

She looked at him. "No. Sheer nosiness."

He nodded. "I like an honest woman. Will you be making a habit of nosiness?"

"I must confess to finding my husband very interesting, and to being possessed of a desire to know him better," Jessie said. "But in the future, I'll be asking him before I snoop."

"That works for me." Zach looked at her. "I should be angry with you, though, right?"

"It was the twins. I admit to feeling jealous."

"They are beautiful," he said, tweaking her, "but just good friends."

"Still, they knew part of you I didn't."

"Ah," he said, "a jealous wife. I'll have to remember that."

"Please do."

"Good. Now get down. Pregnant women shouldn't climb stairs, and you seem to be making a habit of perching on my top attic step."

"Are you mad that I read it?" Jessie asked.

"No. You're my wife. Read what you like in my house. I have some *Playboy*s in the closet—"

"I'm tossing them," she said. "A pregnant wife does not want to feel upstaged by young, skinny women."

He laughed. "I'm teasing. My parents would have made us paint a water tower or something if we'd kept reading material like that on hand, even though the articles are good." He winked at her.

Jessie didn't know what to think about this playful side of her husband. "Thank you for not being mad at me."

"Thank you for being honest. Why'd you choose now to tell me?"

"I have attics of my own that needed cleaning," she said. "I want us to start fresh."

"Babe, we're pretty durn fresh. We just got married."

"I couldn't hide it from you any longer," Jessie said. "I'm beginning to realize how much considering your family members' feelings means."

"That's my girl. Although don't think that Duke, Pepper, and I don't get inconsiderate at times."

"I think you're avoiding your tree," Jessie said, and Zach raised a brow.

"I haven't been much in the mood," he admitted.

"Zach, when I read that first page of your book, I saw us in your writing."

"You couldn't have. It took me three years to write the damn thing. Or if you were there, you're clairvoyant." He came down the ladder and put it up. "Jessie, I'm too simple of a guy to be able to have a relationship and plot a book around it. I swear."

She felt so much better. "Because I thought, you know, the part about—"

"I know. Him marrying her because he had to, and he had all these deep reasons." He tugged her hair. "Do you think pregnancy hormones might be making you jump to conclusions?" Taking her by the hand, he led her into the living room.

"I'm sentimental by nature," Jessie said, as he stood her in front of the tree. "At least, I seem to be becoming more and more sentimental. But you have to admit cleaning a cold attic in the winter when there's four days till Christmas and a warm living room with an undressed tree seems a bit turned around. I thought it might be because of me."

"Oh, you have me turned around," he admitted, "but the tree thing has nothing to do with you. It's the fact that it's just me keeping the home fires burning, and Duke has always teased me about loving to decorate. Now that he's not at the ranch as much, I've lost the motivation of him tweaking me about it. I may have decorated just to get negative attention," he said with a grin. "I liked getting under my big bro's skin."

"I don't believe a word of it," Jessie said. "Look at these happy children."

Zach nodded, looking at the ornament picture. "That's why I was going through the boxes looking for old photographs. I want to be the kind of father my dad was to me. I want my kids to know the happiness we knew growing up." He took a deep breath. "I'm pretty nervous about being a father, to be honest. I guess I was just looking to the past for the right pattern."

She wrapped him in a tight embrace. "I think we're going to make it, Zach."

"Six months isn't that long," he said, and Jessie's heart fell. She'd meant forever, and he was talking about their original plan. It seemed so long ago that they'd agreed to marrying for the children to be born on the right side of the blanket, under his name. Jessie bit her lip. *Great. How honest can I be without upsetting our original agreement?* Would he feel deceived if she told him that she wanted more than what they'd agreed to?

How did you tell a man you'd fallen in love with him if he hadn't told you?

The sound of caroling wafted into the living room. She glanced up at Zach. "Carolers? Is this a tradition in Tulips?"

"Not that I know of," he said.

They peered out into the darkness. Truck headlights illuminated the carolers' path, but they still couldn't see who it was. Together they walked onto the porch, grinning at Helen, Pansy, Bug and Hiram all perched in the back of a truck, singing at the top of their lungs.

"Merry Christmas!" Pansy called.

"Come take your cookie basket," Helen said, holding one up with a big red bow.

Zach walked forward to take it from her. "Who came up with this idea?"

They laughed, their faces aglow and their eyes twinkling in the cold night. "We're starting a tradition," Helen said. "You're our first visit of the night."

"We like it," Jessie said, and Pansy clapped her hands.

"Join us!" Pansy said. "The more, the merrier!"

Zach grinned. "Where are you going next?"

"Liberty's," Hiram said. "She'll have to tuck in early because of the young'un so we want to get her place out of the way next. But y'all were the honeymooners, so we had to bother you first!"

Zach looked at Jessie. "What do you think?"

"Well," she said, "I think there's no room in that truck for us. We'd have to follow you."

"In your tulip-mobile!" Pansy exclaimed. "We've got extra ribbon to put a bow on the grille!" She hopped out of the truck with ribbon. "Bug, you're finally going to get your parade."

"Hot damn, I am!" His face lit up even brighter. "Thank you, Jessie Forrester, I've always wanted a parade."

She blinked at the sound of her name spoken with Zach's last name, realizing she liked it.

Realizing she wanted to keep it more than anything.

"I'll get your keys," Zach said, and Jessie smiled.

"You drive," she said.

The carolers clapped, and Jessie fell in love a little bit more with all things Tulips.

Chapter Eighteen

Being part of a small-town parade was more fun than a cosmetics convention any day, Jessie thought as she sat next to Zach as he drove. They followed the truck in front of them, and Zach had put the top down so they could sing when they got to Liberty and Duke's.

"This is so exciting!" Jessie exclaimed. "Our first tradition."

Zach laughed. "I have to admit, you are not the woman I met. You were so fancy back then you would never have ridden in a pretend parade to make an old man happy."

Jessie shook her head. "Then I wouldn't have known what I was missing."

He reached over and put his hand on her leg. "There may not be much to miss out on in Tulips, but we do manage to stay fairly busy."

"I know." She liked that. Her parents would never understand this, and Jessie knew her life had changed too much for her to ever go back. She would call them one day as Helen and Pansy had suggested in their recipe, but right now, she needed her life to be about Zach.

She hoped he felt the same about her.

They stopped at Liberty's house and cranked up the volume on "Jingle Bells," their voices loud as they huddled together near the porch.

Liberty and Duke opened the door with their baby in Duke's arms.

"Ho, ho, ho," Duke said.

"Merry Christmas, Sheriff," Hiram called. "We're going to Holt's next. Wanna come with us?"

He shook his head. "Baby likes her bath and crib and Santa Mouse story about this time. Come in and let us give you carolers some hot chocolate."

"Mmm," Pansy said, quick to hug Liberty and head inside.

"Let me hold the tiny elf," Helen said, taking the baby from Duke. Liberty smiled at Jessie as she walked onto the porch.

"You look wonderful," Liberty said. "Pregnancy agrees with you."

"And I'm glad about that," Jessie said, laughing.

"Come on in out of the cold." She took Jessie inside and closed the door before following the carolers down the hall to the kitchen. "How'd you get caught up with the Gang?"

"It was easy. They came to our house first and we jumped at the chance to join in the fun." Liberty took Jessie's coat, laying it over a chair. "Zach and I needed some excitement."

Liberty smiled. "It sounds like you've been having plenty of excitement. I heard you sent back the diamond ring Zach got you because it wasn't quite what you wanted."

Jessie felt her smile turn unsteady. "Diamond ring?"

"Your engagement ring?" Liberty looked at her curiously. "You wanted something different, so you all decided to wait until after Christmas to pick one out together?" Liberty gasped at the astonished look on Jessie's face. "Obviously, I'm speaking out of turn, and I pride myself on not being a gossip. Jessie, I'm so sorry!"

Jessie felt weaker than she wanted to but she shook her head. "It's fine. Truly, Liberty."

"Oh, dear." Liberty looked at her, genuinely distressed. "All of us knew about it, so I assumed it was true."

Zach had never mentioned getting her a diamond ring. They'd chosen simple gold bands because they'd agreed on brevity and plainness for a temporary wedding. "I wouldn't send something back that Zach gave me," she said dully. "Liberty, please don't mention to anyone that I didn't know about the diamond."

"I won't!" Liberty promised. "I truly apologize for my runaway mouth."

"No, it's fine," Jessie said, following her into the kitchen. Zach had obviously changed his mind about something concerning her. Jessie's heart shattered into small bits, and when he put his arm around her shoulders in Liberty's cozy, warm kitchen, Jessie wanted to tell him not to bother to put on the good show.

No wonder he hadn't decorated the tree. He wasn't planning on them celebrating a Christmas with all the trimmings.

ON THE NIGHT before Christmas, Jessie placed three presents under the tree. She'd thought about what Liberty had said—a lot—and decided it was up to her to have Christmas.

Maybe the spirit of Christmas would work its wonders on them.

She'd bought a gift for each baby and made one for Zach. For the babies, she'd sentimentally bought booties.

Remembering the flower Zach had made her—and knowing how he had parenting worries—she made him a painted T-shirt that read *World's Best Dad* on the front, and *Love, The Christmas Twins* on the back.

She was pleased with her gifts. She hoped Zach would be, too.

She intended to celebrate Christmas as if this one were the first of many they'd spend together.

But for now, she had a difficult phone call to make and she couldn't put it off any longer.

ZACH HAD PLANS—big plans. He didn't know how Jessie would react to them, but it was time to find out.

He found her sitting with the phone in her hands.

"What are you doing?"

"About to sweep cobwebs," she said.

He thought she'd never looked more beautiful, which made his plan all the more important. "Anything I can help with?"

She shook her head. "Not this time."

He sat beside her. "Want some company? Or privacy?"

She thought about that for a long time. "I really don't know," she said, so he kissed her to make her feel better. It was all he had to give her. She clung to him for a moment, and then broke away.

He missed her already. "Tomorrow's Christmas," he said, and she looked at him.

"I know."

"I'm glad you're here."

She nodded. "I am, too."

"I'm not going to ever submit my western."

"You're not? Why not?"

"It's not something I need to do anymore. I always wanted to write a book, so I wrote a book to see if I could. But the challenge isn't the kind of excitement I need. I've got you and that's enough."

"I wish that sounded complimentary."

He kissed her forehead. "It is. Should I dial for you?"

"I never thanked you for calling my folks. It means a lot to me, more than I expressed at the time."

He nodded. "I felt it was important."

Slowly, she dialed the number, and he sat down beside her. "Mother?"

He put his hand over Jessie's.

"Mother, I'm calling to tell you and Dad Merry Christmas. I'm sorry you don't trust me enough to make my own decisions and know my own mind, but I've accepted that. I love you, and I want you to be happy. So Merry Christmas, and that's all I called to say."

Zach held his breath. Jessie listened for a long time, her eyes beginning to sparkle with tears, so he handed her a tissue, and then she smiled, her whole face lighting up. "I love you, too," she said. "Zach will be delighted."

She hung up. "You're never going to believe this. My parents have had a change of heart, and they want to know if you'll mind if they come to Tulips for the birth of the children in May or whenever it happens."

He slowly shook his head, his eyes taking in Jessie's joy. "Of course not. Your family is welcome anytime."

"She said to tell you she was sorry. She and Dad panicked."

"I actually understand. I probably would have, too, had I been in their shoes."

"You have a big heart," she said, putting her arms around his neck. "The biggest in Texas."

"I don't know about that." He stroked her hair. "I'm glad you and your family worked everything out. It bothered me more than I can tell you that I was the cause of so much distress for you."

She pulled away to look at him. "Zach, I never doubted that you and I had made the right decision."

They sat together for a long time, holding each other and feeling the magic of Christmas wash over them. And when he got up and began to clean out her room, Jessie helped him, and together, they moved her up to his bedroom where she belonged.

ON CHRISTMAS MORNING, she heard Zach rustling around downstairs. She felt the bed beside her, where she'd slept snuggled up against him in his arms all night.

It had been so incredible, the best gift she could have gotten. He'd cradled her stomach in his big hands and she felt she'd come home for good.

But it was Christmas, and she wasn't going to let him start it without her. Hurriedly dressing, she flew downstairs and jumped into his arms. "Merry Christmas, husband!"

Zach laughed out loud, loving Jessie's spontaneity. She certainly wasn't a wife who would allow him to become bored. "Merry Christmas to you, too, wife."

Jessie gasped, looking at the tree he'd sneaked downstairs to decorate for her. "Pretty good, huh?"

"It's beautiful!" She smiled, delighted.

"You got me started." He pointed to the photo ornament.

"I'm glad. Have you finished? Or are there more?"

"There's a few more in that box. And this one," Zach said. "It's a special one. Please be careful when you open the box."

"Oh, I will." Jessie carefully unwrapped the family heirloom that had been kept in a red, velvet-lined box. She held up a gold carved heart-shaped ornament. "It's so beautiful."

"It even opens," he said, showing her how to unhinge it, and Jessie gasped when she saw the beautiful diamond ring inside.

He grinned, liking how he'd surprised her. "Merry Christmas, Jessie Tomball Farnsworth Forrester. Will you marry me and be my wife—forever?"

She threw herself into her arms. "Yes! Oh, Zach, it's beautiful!"

He held her close. "I love you, girl. I loved you the moment I laid eyes on you."

"I have waited so long to hear you say those words, so I could tell you I love you, too." Jessie kissed him softly on the mouth. "I love you more than I ever believed I could love someone."

"We'll have to have another wedding here, you know," Zach said, his eyes twinkling, "because the Gang felt slighted, though they tried to be supportive. Liberty wants to design you a dress, and the ladies want to get Valentine to bring a wedding cake over from Union Junction."

"And my family could come," she said on a hopeful breath, and he nodded.

"I already called your father and asked him for your hand in marriage, and this time, he said yes." Zach grinned.

"I bet Dad was impressed by your courage."

"I was more impressed by the fact that he tore up the documents he'd had me sign." Zach shrugged. "He said you had the brightest mind of any woman he'd ever known besides your mother, and if you chose me, then I was the man to make you happy."

Jessie began to cry tears of joy. "Thank you for being such a prince," she said.

"Thank you for being you," he replied, pulling her up into his lap. Together, they sat and watched the twinkling lights on the tree sparkling on the many ornaments, and the spirit of the season glowed like candlelight on them and the babies that had brought them together.

Epilogue

One Christmas Eve later, Jessie got the chance to relive her holiday miracle. She married Zach in a sweet ceremony in Tulips, allowing Pansy, Helen, Liberty and Pepper to celebrate her wedding the way they'd always wanted.

Jessie had been satisfied with their elopement, but as far as the Gang was concerned, if they hadn't witnessed the ceremony, the marriage wasn't completely perfect. And nothing could be more wonderful than a wedding surrounded by your friends and family, they explained, and so Jessie relaxed and enjoyed their surprise nuptials.

It hadn't been a surprise to Zach. These days, anything the Gang wanted to do he was amenable to. Liberty had designed Jessie a lovely wedding gown, and the ladies had decorated the parlor at the Triple F. They'd invited Jessie's family, and this time, even her brothers had shown up to watch her father give her away. It had been a very special Christmas wedding, and Jessie loved Zach even more for understanding how much it meant to her.

Her husband had turned out to be quite the conspirator, she decided, smiling at him as he cooed at baby Mattie lying in his arms. In May, when the babies had been born, he'd allowed the Gang to hang balloons and streamers all over the house as a baby welcome. Two giant wooden storks had been posted on the lawn, announcing the children's names and birth weights. The storks' faces had been covered over by photographs, one of Zach and one of Jessie on each. They looked ridiculous with human faces, and Jessie had laughed out loud when Zach drove her home from the hospital and she saw them for the first time.

"So, wife, our children are seven months old and look as if they understand there are presents under the tree for them," Zach said as he stood in front of the tree which, this year, had been decorated the day after Halloween. He said the children needed to learn about family, friends and holiday baking as soon as possible, though Jessie was certain Zach was eager to slip into his Santa role more than anything. He was wearing a Santa cap right now and was gazing at the twins like he'd received the most wonderful gift of all.

Jessie snuggled James to her cheek. "If they love the holidays half as much as their father, we'll always have a lot of excitement this time of year. I can't believe they're seven months old."

"Yes, a very important birthday," he said, kissing James's head and then Jessie on the lips. "But more importantly, it's our first Christmas as a family."

She smiled. "You're right."

"Next year, the babies will actually sing when we ride around caroling."

"I can't wait."

"I'm glad we got married again today," he told her. "The babies knew something special was happening."

She put her arm through his, and the babies looked at the lights glowing on the tree. "When I first met you that day on the road, I thought you were such a tough guy. And here you are, sentimental and sweet. I would never have guessed."

"You only thought I was tough because you'd hit my prize steer. If a woman ever hits your steer, James—"

"You'd best love her with all your heart,"

Jessie said, laughing. "Brahma Bud likes me better than you now."

"Only because you take him daily treats to atone for your poor driving skills."

Jessie laughed. "Mattie, if ever you meet a man who wants to seduce you in the back of your T-bird—"

"I'll not be buying my daughter a hot pink car," Zach said. "She'll be riding a bicycle for the rest of her life."

"You know," Jessie said, looking up at him, "when she falls in love, there'll be very little you can do about it."

Zach gazed down into Jessie's eyes. "If and when I allow my children to have a date with the opposite sex, I hope they're as happy as I am with you."

Happiness shone in Jessie's eyes. "I love you, Zach."

He kissed her lips and each baby flailed a fist, making their parents laugh. Jessie leaned her head against Zach's shoulder as they stood silently looking at the tree, holding their future in their arms, letting the magic of the holidays bless their marriage forever.

It was fairy-tale perfect, and only the beginning of their story.

* * * * *

*Turn the page for a sneak peek at the next book
in THE TULIPS SALOON miniseries,
HER SECRET SONS,
coming March 2007
only from Harlequin American Romance.*

Men were Pepper Forrester's downfall—and salvation.

For the past thirteen years Pepper had lived away from Tulips in the north with her Aunt Jerry, bringing up her twin sons. She had two brothers, Zach and Duke, both happy to disrupt her life, although mostly with charm and well-meaning opinions. These four males were the most important people in her world. Her salvation.

The twins' father—the man responsible for seducing her out of her good sense and virginity—was Luke McGarrett, the only man she'd ever loved. Why it had to be him was an obvious, yet, painful answer: he'd been glib, sexy, hot. She'd said yes—and therefore he'd been her downfall.

But that was the past. She'd needed a plan to

bring closure to her life, so she picked June for her return to Tulips, Texas, to confess the secret she'd kept all these years—she had done her own bit to increase the town's population on the sly.

Hopefully, no one would suspect Luke was the father.

She comforted herself by thinking about how Luke went off after high school to find his way in the world, never to be seen again, and heard from infrequently.

Pepper packed the last box, looking around at the place where she and the twins had lived for the past thirteen years. Tulips was home sweet home, but her brothers were going to be mad and hurt that she'd kept their nephews from them. They'd been adamantly opposed to their own women having a baby without them—no children of theirs would be unaware of who their father was. Out of all the Forresters, she was the one who'd done just that. But she wasn't proud of it.

The citizens of Tulips thought she was such a smart and responsible person.

Pansy Trifle and Helen Granger, members of the Tulips Saloon Gang and some of their dearest friends, would be shocked. Bug Carmine and Hiram Parsons, two of the local men who kept

Tulips running, would have plenty of thoughts on the matter.

She dreaded the confession. Thirteen years wasn't long enough for people's memories to fade. She'd been a bright-eyed girl who'd recently lost her parents, and Luke had been her hero. She'd fallen in love with so much fever and need that still, after all these years, she wished their relationship had been more than a high-school dream.

Too bad he'd turned out to be such a rat.

Pepper had been studious, determined to get into college and then medical school. Her Aunt Jerry loved her in spite of everything, and helped her out with the twins while Pepper went to school. She felt guilty for keeping the boys from their father but Luke had never returned to Tulips, not even for a holiday. That salved her conscience somewhat.

She'd recently purchased a house in Tulips, which she'd converted into a clinic for the small town. It was her way of giving back to the people who had taken such good care of her over the years; it was her way of returning with grace and honor and hope for belonging.

"Come on, boys," she said, "it's time to go home."

"I guess you're sure this is the right thing to do," Toby complained.

"No. I'm not." She locked the door. "But I have my own clinic and so we're moving where my job and your family is."

"They don't feel like family. Aunt Jerry is family."

Duke and Zach might never forgive her for this, considering how they felt about women keeping their children from them. "Aunt Jerry may come live in Tulips next year."

"Really?" Both boys perked up.

They all got in the car, and Pepper nodded. "I think so. After I have some time to get us settled."

"So…will our father be there?"

Pepper swallowed hard. "No. He never went back to Tulips. I don't know where he is. I'm sorry." They shrugged. "I love you both so much," she said as two sad faces looked out the window, saying their goodbyes to the only home they'd ever known.

"People are going to make fun of us. The kids are going to know we don't have a father," Josh said.

"I don't think that will happen. I believe you'll be embraced with open arms. It's me whom everyone is going to be a little surprised by, but—" she took a deep breath "—I never said I was perfect. And you guys are my saving graces. My life is good because of you."

They noted that with silence, and Pepper didn't begrudge them their mood. At least she didn't have to face the one thing she probably never could: Luke McGarrett. From him, she was safe.

Luke McGarret helped three women onto the luxury yacht with his typical courteous smile. Then he assisted their father, the general, on board as well, scanning the landscape to make certain they weren't being followed by paparazzi, mischief-makers or beggars.

It was a tough life having to guard beautiful leggy blondes every day of his life, but someone had to do it, he thought with a grin. Being a world traveler and in the employ of the general definitely had its rewards, mainly the scenery.

The scenery was untouchable, of course, since they were his job, but he had to admit he wasn't attracted to the girls. If anything, he was attracted to the traveling and the money and the fact that he'd never have to return to Tulips, Texas.

He sat at the stern once everyone was seated and pulled a letter from his inside shirt pocket to reread.

Luke,
You've been gone a long time. I know we've had our differences but I'm getting older and

need some help with the family real estate business. I'd like my only son to learn my profession and I'd like to spend some time getting to know you. I've missed that.
Love, Dad

Luke put the letter away, resisting the urge to toss it into the sea. There was nothing in Tulips for him. He didn't care about a family business. The last thing he was ever going to do was find a wife and settle down and start having kids—and he knew very well that was on his father's mind. *Oh, no, sir, not me. I'm single and proud of it.*

* * * * *

New York Times *bestselling author Linda Lael Miller is back with a new romance featuring the heartwarming McKettrick family from Silhouette Special Edition.*

SIERRA'S HOMECOMING
by Linda Lael Miller

On sale December 2006,
wherever books are sold.

Turn the page for a sneak preview!

Soft, smoky music poured into the room.

The next thing she knew, Sierra was in Travis's arms, close against that chest she'd admired earlier, and they were slow dancing.

Why didn't she pull away?

"Relax," he said. His breath was warm in her hair.

She giggled, more nervous than amused. What was the matter with her? She was attracted to Travis, had been from the first, and he was clearly attracted to her. They were both adults. Why not enjoy a little slow dancing in a ranch-house kitchen?

Because slow dancing led to other things. She took a step back and felt the counter flush against her lower back. Travis naturally came with her, since they were holding hands and he had one arm around her waist.

Simple physics.

Then he kissed her.

Physics again—this time, not so simple.

"Yikes," she said, when their mouths parted.

He grinned. "Nobody's ever said that after I kissed them."

She felt the heat and substance of his body pressed against hers. "It's going to happen, isn't it?" she heard herself whisper.

"Yep," Travis answered.

"But not tonight," Sierra said on a sigh.

"Probably not," Travis agreed.

"When, then?"

He chuckled, gave her a slow, nibbling kiss. "Tomorrow morning," he said. "After you drop Liam off at school."

"Isn't that…a little…soon?"

"Not soon enough," Travis answered, his voice husky. "Not nearly soon enough."

REQUEST YOUR FREE BOOKS!
2 FREE NOVELS PLUS 2
FREE GIFTS!

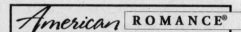

Heart, Home & Happiness!

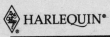
HARLEQUIN®

American ROMANCE®

IS PROUD TO PRESENT

COWBOY VET
by Pamela Britton

Jessie Monroe is the last person on earth Rand Sheppard wants to rely on, but he needs a veterinary technician—yesterday—and she's the only one for hire. It turns out the woman who destroyed his cousin's life isn't who Rand thought she was. And now she's all he can think about!

"Pamela Britton writes the kind of wonderfully romantic, sexy, witty romance that readers dream of discovering when they go into a bookstore."

—*New York Times* bestselling author
Jayne Ann Krentz

**Cowboy Vet *is available from
Harlequin American Romance in December 2006.***

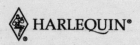

HARLEQUIN®

American ROMANCE®

COMING NEXT MONTH

#1141 A LARAMIE, TEXAS CHRISTMAS by Cathy Gillen Thacker
The McCabes: Next Generation
All Kevin McCabe wants for Christmas is to get closer to Noelle Kringle.
She and her son are in Laramie for the holidays, and he finds himself strongly
attracted to her. He can tell the feeling is mutual, but as quickly as Kevin's
falling in love, he can't help but wonder what it is she's trying to hide.

#1142 TEMPTED BY A TEXAN by Mindy Neff
Texas Sweethearts
Becca Sue Ellsworth's prospects for cuddling a child of her own seem grim,
until the night her old flame arrives first on the scene of a break-in to rescue her
from a prowler. Suddenly she realizes she has another chance to get Colby Flynn
to rethink his ambition to be a big-city lawyer—and to remind the long, tall
Texan of a baby-making promise seven years ago…the one she'd gotten from him!

#1143 COWBOY VET by Pamela Britton
Jessie Monroe is the last person on earth Rand Sheppard wants to rely on, but
he needs a veterinary technician—yesterday—and she's the only one for hire.
It turns out the woman who destroyed his cousin's life isn't who Rand thought
she was. And now she's all he can think about….

#1144 THE WEDDING SECRET by Michele Dunaway
American Beauties
After landing a plum position on the hottest talk show in the country,
Cecile Duletsky is ready for just about anything. Anything but gorgeous
Luke Shaw, that is. Cecile spends a fabulous night with him, knowing she isn't
ready for a complicated romance. But that's before she shows up for work and
finds Luke—her boss—sitting across from her in the boardroom.

www.eHarlequin.com

HARCNM1106